RANGELAND RUCKUS

Chet Mitchell's dream was to raise cattle, near the town of Tanning, in a seemingly inaccessible valley. However, landowner Dave Tanning didn't want strangers to ranch land that he felt belonged to his family. And people laughed at Chet's plan to access the valley, which was surrounded by mountains and enormous rock walls. Many had tried, and died. But when Mitchell unveiled his surprise, Dave Tanning had to face a man who knew how to use his head and his guns . . .

RANDALL SAWKA

RANGELAND
RUCKUS

Complete and Unabridged

LINFORD
Leicester

First published in Great Britain in 2008 by
Robert Hale Limited, London

First Linford Edition
published 2009
by arrangement with
Robert Hale Limited, London

British Library CIP Data

Sawka, Randall.
    Rangeland ruckus - -
    (Linford western library)
    1. Western stories.
    2. Large type books.
    I. Title II. Series
    823.9'2–dc22

    ISBN 978–1–84782–853–8

Published by
F. A. Thorpe (Publishing)
Anstey, Leicestershire

Set by Words & Graphics Ltd.
Anstey, Leicestershire
Printed and bound in Great Britain by
T. J. International Ltd., Padstow, Cornwall

This book is printed on acid-free paper

1

Dusk tinted the sky red as Chet Mitchell stopped at the crest of the hill above the town of Tanning. The tall, lean man pulled off his flat-topped hat and wiped his brow with his red bandanna. The tail of his tall roan swept back and forth in the evening heat. The trailing mule looked up wearily, its mottled coat covered in dust from the day's ride over the springtime rangeland.

Mitchell looked up and smiled as the remainder of the sun's light flooded over the distant mountains. The triangle of rough mountains, known locally as the Three Points, had drawn him to the area and now concealed his future. Legend had it that over twenty men had died trying to find a good trail in to the lush triangular valley between the mountains. Towering rock faces stood like castle walls between the points. None could find a way to get cattle to the swaying grass and take advantage of the clear spring water in the meandering rivers and creeks that wound through the valley.

Legend also stated that a few people, mostly Indians, had found their way to the spot. They had entered the valley through a narrow crack in one of the forty-foot thick walls. The passage, just wide enough for a man to squeeze through, led them on to a tight path filled with jagged rocks and rough ground.

Chet Mitchell had spent years in the gold-mining camps of California. He'd worked long hard days on his claim to earn enough money to finance a cattle ranch. One day a man who'd heard about Chet's calm efficient way with dynamite hired him to do some blasting. Soon Mitchell spent less time on his claim and more time hiring out his services for the dangerous and lucrative job of handling explosives. His bankroll had grown rapidly and now he focused on his dream of settling down and raising cattle.

In the small mining area where he had been born, a young Chet Mitchell had seen his parents gunned down in cold blood, the killers after their pouch of gold. Chet had escaped death because his father had pushed him behind some bushes as the thieves approached. His uncle had buried Chet's parents and raised the young man in the gold-mining area.

When Chet turned thirteen his uncle had reached into a high cupboard and pulled out a holster and two heavy old Colt revolvers. The weapons were well maintained and oiled, the handles worn. His uncle had been an excellent shot but had hung up the guns years before. The boy strapped on the guns, which hung low on his thin frame. His uncle tossed him two boxes of bullets and took him out into a ravine where he taught him how to shoot. The boy was a natural and soon the revolvers became a fixture around his waist.

The rumors of the mysterious and inaccessible valley spread to the mining area. Never afraid of a challenge, this one literally mountain high, Chet dreamed of ranching the valley and making it his home.

A quick tap on the side of the roan and the horse moved down the hill. The mule, its head bobbing, followed reluctantly. The town's main street contained several saloons and hotels. A general store and barber shop stood across the street from the livery stable. Men standing outside the saloons and walking along the boardwalks looked the stranger over carefully. They saw his twin tied-down Colts and powerful horse. Mitchell rode up to the trough in front of the livery stable and let the horse and mule drink deeply. A boy ran out of the stable, his neck craned to make eye contact with the tall stranger.

Mitchell tossed the boy a coin. 'Give them a good rubdown and some oats.'

'Yes, sir, I'll do it right away,' said the

boy, as he looked disbelievingly at the coin, equal to a day's pay.

Chet dismounted and walked along the covered board-walk. He glanced at the sign above each business as he passed, all named after the town's creator and richest citizen, Dave Tanning. Tanning not only owned most of the town but also most of the land surrounding it.

Mitchell had only stopped in Tanning once before to pick up supplies before heading off to explore the Three Points and the hidden valley behind them. The reception at the hotel and general store had been cool on that visit. They had treated strangers with caution, asking probing questions about the reason for the visit. The man at the general store had surveyed the items purchased by Mitchell and had asked his plans. Chet had indicated he was passing through, knowing that any information he gave would be in the hands of Dave Tanning within an hour. After loading the supplies on the pack mule Mitchell had mounted his roan and slowly moved along the rutted street.

Others had also shown interest in Mitchell's movements. Men had leaned against the wall of the hotel with their hats pulled down, throwing shadows over their eyes. Chet had caught each of them glancing at him through the sides of their eyes as he passed. Once out of sight Chet had hidden his horse and mule behind some trees and slipped back into town. He slid up the dark passage between the barber shop and the saloon, where he watched the men from the street and the storekeeper gather in a circle before walking into Dave Tanning's office. Mitchell had confirmed his suspicion that Tanning was a man of great power.

Mitchell then left town the same way he had entered, in the opposite direction to the Three Points. The wind was welcome as it had quickly obscured his tracks and he knew he had time to implement his plan before the locals or Tanning heard about it.

The people in the area, especially Tanning with all his thirsty cattle, kept close watch on the Three Points as this was the source of much of the water that flowed in the rivers and creeks that fed their rich grazing land.

On this second visit Chet first stopped in at the barber shop, as he needed to clean up after so many months in the wilderness. The hot bath removed layers of dust. Smoke from Chet's fine cigar wafted through the shop as he soaked in the large tub. The barber cut his hair and gave him a close shave while putting Mitchell through the usual line of questioning.

'Don't recall seeing you in Tanning before,' said the barber as he trimmed the back of Chet's hair.

'Can't imagine you did, seeing that this is my first time in your chair.'

'Passing through, I suppose.'

'Might, or I might stick around for a bit. Just don't know.'

'Uh-huh. Well, there you are, stranger. All done.'

Mitchell studied himself in the large mirror behind the chair. His ruggedly handsome face with its square jaw was darkly tanned from months of working in the hot sun, climbing and reclimbing the Three Points looking for a passage into the valley. Mitchell straightened the collar on his fresh shirt and put on his hat. He checked himself in the mirror one last time, barely recognizing himself as the same grimy man who had ridden into town two hours earlier. He set four bits on the counter and grabbed the door handle.

Chet walked out of the barbershop and slowly made his way up the street until he reached the general store where he had stopped on his previous visit to the town. He didn't bother looking back, but knew that the barber was probably already on his way to Tanning's office to pass on what little he'd learned from the stranger. Mitchell pushed open the door and walked across the wooden floor to the counter.

The shopkeeper looked up nervously

from his newspaper. 'Well, you're back, just like you said.'

'Yup. I told you I was expecting a delivery and here I am.'

'Sure, sure. I got it right here.' The shopkeeper straightened his spectacles and pulled a piece of paper out from under the counter.

'Says here the package came from California and to keep it in a cool place.' The man pointed to the back room of the store. 'I got it back there. I'll get it for you.'

Chet stood quietly while the shopkeeper scurried into the back. He returned shortly, struggling with the heavy box. Chet touched it and found the wood cool.

'Told you, coldest place in the store; in town for that matter,' said the storekeeper as he looked back at the paperwork. 'That totals three dollars including the storage charges.'

'That's fine.' Mitchell dropped three one-dollar coins on the counter and handed the shopkeeper a list. 'I need these things as well.'

The shopkeeper put the order together while Chet inspected the box closely. The heavy-duty lock remained in place, but he noticed scratch marks as though someone had tried to open it. He knew the lock was tamperproof so he looked over the rest of the box. A small smile crossed his face when he noticed the futile pry marks on one corner of the reinforced metal lid. Chet pulled out a key and opened the lock. He lifted the lid slightly and saw the thin, folded brown paper that he had glued between the box bottom and the lid. It was still in place. He had packed the box in California before he left and made arrangements to have it shipped out to Tanning a few months later. He now knew that only he knew the contents of the box.

Chet relocked the box and crossed the floor of the store to where the storekeeper was weighing a pound of coffee. 'Can you hold the box and the rest of these supplies in the cool area in the back? I'll pick them up in the morning.'

'They'll be ready, stranger,' said the storekeeper. 'Those are fine old guns. What's that on the handles?'

'Golden eagles.'

'Eagles, huh. Interesting.'

'To some,' said Chet as he walked out the door of the store.

As Mitchell reached halfway down the street he heard keys rattling behind him, followed by the scurry of boots. He glanced in the reflection of the hotel's window and saw the storekeeper rushing across the street in the direction of Tanning's office.

Mitchell grinned and pushed open the door to the hotel. He crossed the small lobby, his shadow covering the young man shuffling papers.

'A room for the night,' said Mitchell.

The innkeeper reached behind him and removed a key from a hook and threw it on the counter in front of Chet. 'Fifty cents: in advance.'

Chet scooped up the key and

replaced it with fifty cents. The young man turned the register around and set a pen on top of it. Mitchell looked at the innkeeper and walked away.

'But, but — ' The plea of the man faded as Mitchell walked away, knowing that the only strangers who signed registers were people who wanted their names known, usually salesmen. Chet had nothing to sell but he had an empty stomach to fill.

The smell of fresh cooking drew Mitchell to the adjoining dining room. The room had a dozen tables but only one was occupied. At it sat a man and a woman who were having an animated conversation. The powerfully-built, serious-looking man wore a gun tied down. The pretty blonde woman seemed determined to have her way and the man didn't like it. Chet set his hat on the chair of a table across the room from the arguing couple. The table gave him a view of the street and the saloon across the street while keeping his back to a wall.

The waitress set a mug on Chet's

table and filled it to the rim. Steam curled into the air over the dark brew.

'Something to eat?' asked the waitress.

'Steak, rare.'

The waitress pushed open a white door and disappeared into the kitchen.

As Mitchell took his first sip of coffee the woman at the table across the room jumped to her feet and put her hands on her hips. Her hair shook as she argued in a low voice with the man. She was attractive and slim. Her rich tan showed that she enjoyed the outdoors and the look on her face showed she was very upset with the man. Her pretty face seemed built for a smile but wore a frown.

The stubbornly argumentative man looked about twenty-five, the same age as Mitchell. He wore expensive clothes and a new hat rested on the chair beside him. His boots also suggested money, well polished but worn on the inside indicating plenty of time in the saddle. While not as tall as Mitchell he had broad shoulders, slim waist, and powerful arms.

As Chet sipped his coffee he heard a chair scrape across the wooden floor.

'Stay, I said!' shouted the man in a louder voice as he jumped out of his chair. 'I mean it.'

'Leave me alone,' replied the woman.

'Just you remember who's in charge here.' The man grabbed for her arm but his fingers only brushed it as she pulled away.

Chet put down his cup and looked up at the couple as she continued to back away from the man. 'Best leave the woman be,' he said.

The man sneered at Mitchell. 'Mind your own business, stranger. You don't know who you're dealing with.'

Chet locked eyes with the man and took another sip of the coffee. 'If you don't behave *I'll* be dealing with *you*.'

'I wouldn't recommend that,' said the man as he jumped forward and gripped the young lady's arm. He looked her square in the eyes. 'Now you and me are leaving, Lisa. Right now.'

Chet sprang out of his chair and across the room. He wrapped his large hand around the man's wrist and squeezed. The man winced as the vise-like grip increased and his hand turned white. He released the woman's arm. She backed away, rubbing her arm.

The man drew back with his left hand and swung at Chet's cheek. Mitchell pulled back smoothly and the punch caught air. Chet continued to hold the man's right arm and jabbed at his jaw. He caught him squarely in the mouth, sending the man falling backwards, crashing into a table before tumbling onto the floor. The man hopped back onto his feet and Mitchell prepared himself for a counter-attack. Instead, the man wiped blood from his bottom lip and backed out the door and onto the street.

'This isn't over, not by a long shot!' shouted the man as the door swung shut. He crossed the street and climbed up the steps on the other side of the street. He grabbed the batwing door as he stomped into the saloon there. The doors nearly flew off their hinges as he threw them backwards once inside the bar.

The young woman also watched the man bolt into the saloon. She cradled her arm as she stood in the corner of the dining room. Chet noticed bruises on her right arm. She looked down as she crossed the dining room toward Chet. She lifted her head and her gaze connected with Mitchell's.

She had a puzzled look on her face and said, 'Thank you, stranger, but you best get out of town. That was Will Tanning you just hit.'

'Kin to Dave Tanning?'

'His youngest son. I suspect the old man and the two older boys won't take kindly to what you did.'

Chet smiled and put on his hat. 'I thank you for your concern, ma'am, but I reckon I can handle them. I've never been one to back away from trouble.'

'I admire your confidence but the Tanning family owns pretty much this whole town. They usually get their way and all four can handle a gun.'

'Beg pardon,' said Chet. 'The name's Mitchell, Chet Mitchell.'

'I'm Lisa Cullen. My pa has a small ranch just this side of the Three Points.'

'Mighty pleased to meet you. I'm new to these parts and hope to find a piece of land and raise some cattle myself.'

'I wish you well, Mr Mitchell, but most of the land in this area is owned by the Tannings and they hold it tight. What little land that is free either doesn't have any water or you can't get to it.'

'Ah, I reckon you're talking about the valley between the Three Points,' said Chet, grinning. 'I heard that was just a legend. Oh, and please call me Chet.'

'Thank you, Chet. Call me Lisa. And it isn't a legend. Why I — ' Lisa looked across the road and saw four men push their way through the doors of the saloon across the street. 'You'd best leave now. That's Will and Dave Tanning. With them are the other sons, Luke and Alan. Oh my, they're heading this way.'

Chet slowly turned his head to look at the four men. He instinctively checked the position of his twin Colts.

'Lisa, you best slip out the back door while I get better acquainted with the Tannings.'

Lisa rushed to the kitchen door and stopped. She glanced back at the tall stranger before disappearing behind the door.

The four men in the street walked side-by-side like soldiers on the march as they stepped over the ruts there. The older man walked with confidence, a stern look on his face. Like his sons he was not a tall man but they were all built powerfully with wide shoulders and narrow waists. As they neared the door to the dining room the three sons hesitated slightly, but Dave Tanning maintained his pace and barged through the door. Over a dozen men spilled out of the saloon onto the street behind the Tannings and followed them at a distance.

Looks like we'll have an audience, thought Chet, sitting at his table against the wall. *So much the better.*

Mitchell slowly sipped coffee with his left hand as Alan and Luke joined their father and Will, blood still dripping from his lip, at the far end of the dining room. Chet's right hand rested on his worn leather holster, inches from his Colt.

Alan, Will and Luke stepped past their father but the older man put up his hands and his sons stopped on the spot.

The waitress stopped clearing the nearby table and moved to the safety of the kitchen.

Dave Tanning stood and sized up the stranger. He looked at his sons, then back at Mitchell.

'I'll handle this,' he whispered, just loud enough to carry to Chet's ears.

Dave Tanning moved two steps closer to Mitchell, who continued to drink his coffee. 'I hear you roughed up my boy.'

Chet looked up and locked eyes with Tanning. 'Seems he doesn't know how to treat a lady. I just took it upon myself to teach him some manners.'

'Nobody tells my boys anything except me. Nobody. Do you understand, mister?'

Mitchell pretended he didn't hear the older man and continued staring him straight in the eye.

Dave Tanning dropped his eyes and studied Mitchell's lean physique and his tied-down colts. 'Stranger, you'd best leave my town.'

'Reckon I like it here. I think I'll stick around for a bit, maybe even raise a few head of cattle.'

'You'll do no such thing,' said Dave Tanning as he backed into line with his sons. 'Boys, I think it's time we showed this stranger what happens when you mess with the Tannings.'

Mitchell sprang to his feet. He drew

and aimed his twin Colts at the four men before they could grip their weapons. 'Seems mighty unneighborly, four against one.'

The buzz of excitement in the growing crowd outside carried through the open doors.

The Tannings slowly raised their hands, a look of shock on the face of the boys, seething anger and embarrassment on their dad's.

'Now, unlike you skunks I'm a fair man. Suppose I slip my guns back in the holsters and make things interesting by trying this again.'

The din from outside grew louder from the now three-deep crowd that had scattered to the sides to avoid stray bullets.

The Tannings looked at each other, then back at Mitchell.

'I can make one promise though,' added Mitchell 'My first shot, and I will get off the first shot, will go straight into the heart of your pa. Based on what I've seen so far I expect to get off the second as well.' Mitchell smiled. 'Why don't we let that one be a surprise?'

Dave Tanning's concerned eyes dug into Mitchell's. 'Alan, Luke, Will, keep your heads about you. We don't want to do anything rash.'

The elder Tanning backed towards the door, his sons following close behind. The group of people outside backed onto the street as the four men moved along the wooden boardwalk. Dave Tanning's glare through the window never left Mitchell until he turned and walked down onto the street. The lamps cast four long shadows as the father and sons walked into the Tanning saloon and disappeared into the crowd.

Chet sat down at his table. He heard the kitchen door open. The waitress peeked out and saw that it was safe to come out. In her right hand was a steaming plate of food, including the thickest steak Mitchell had ever seen. The waitress grinned as she watched the Tanning men skulk away.

'I'd say that calls for a refill of coffee,' she said, as she filled the cup with the hot brew.

Chet cut a piece of the steak and popped it in his mouth. 'Mighty fine steak.'

'Best cut I could find. Some of us don't like the way the Tannings push everyone around.'

The first bite of food reminded Chet of his hunger and he methodically devoured the rest of the meal. After one more cup of coffee he paid for the meal and left a healthy tip.

The young man behind the desk in the lobby was chatting with another man. They abruptly stopped their animated conversation when Mitchell entered and started up the creaking wooden stairs leading to the second floor. As he rounded the corner he heard the muffled voices start up again.

Chet pulled out his left-side Colt and turned the key in the lock with his right hand. He slowly opened the door and saw that he was alone in the small, sparsely furnished room. He closed the gap in the curtains and prepared himself for his first sleep in a real bed in weeks. A Colt rested on the bedside table pointing towards the door. He stretched out on the bed and fell asleep within a minute of his head hitting the feather pillow.

In the Tanning saloon Dave Tanning sat in his usual chair at the poker table. He studied the faces of his four opponents. Each, including him, had taken one card. Tanning missed his flush but bet heavily anyways, knowing that his wealth dwarfed the combined holdings of all four men. The first man folded quickly. The second man did as well. The third man, a regular at the table, stared at Tanning and then back at his cards. When Tanning saw him scratch his chin he knew he was beat.

'I raise another twenty.' The man threw two bills into the center of the table.

'Ah, take it,' said Tanning as he

tossed his cards on the table and scooped up the remainder of his money.

The other man tried but failed to hide his pleasure. He knew Tanning's mind was not on his game and that he had reaped the reward.

The three Tanning boys stood at the bar. They were the only ones drinking the expensive whiskey. The talk in the saloon was in lowered voices, undoubtedly about the new man in town with hands the speed of lightning. It wasn't the first fast gun to pass through Tanning but it was the first to humble the Tanning family.

'I've never seen guns like that before,' said Will Tanning. 'Them old Colts had gold birds on the handles.'

'Birds on the handles, you say?' asked Nugget Rimmer, an old man with a long gray beard sitting alone at a nearby table. 'What kind of birds?' Rimmer spat tobacco into the spittoon at the end of the bar.

The three brothers looked at Rimmer, surprised because the old man seldom talked, let alone started a conversation.

'They were eagles, Nugget.' replied Alan. 'Why do you ask?'

The only thing more rare than Nugget Rimmer talking was Nugget Rimmer laughing, but the old man roared with laughter until he choked.

He swallowed a mouthful of beer to ease the pain. 'It appears you don't know who you was up against.'

Will Tanning leaned forward. 'And you do, old man?'

'Seems so.' Beer ran down his matted beard as he drained his glass and put it on the table in front of the Tannings. 'But I could think better with another cold beer in front of me.'

The Tanning sons moved toward the old man who sat smugly in his chair with a toothless grin on his face. Dave Tanning gripped the shoulders of his two sons with callused hands.

'Easy boys. Let's hear what the old-timer has to say.' Tanning got a beer from the bartender and set it in front of Rimmer. He then took a seat at the table. The boys stood behind the elder Tanning, all waiting impatiently for the old man.

Rimmer sipped his beer. 'Obliged. I hope those two boys of yours don't intend on beating on an old man.'

Dave Tanning smiled. 'I promise I'll keep them away. Now you just tell us what you know about that man calling himself Mitchell.'

'Right. When I first heard about those Colts I had a feeling that I recognized them. But when I heard the man's name that cinched it. I first saw those old Colts with the gold eagles on another man named Mitchell. However, he was much older than this youngster you're talking about. I tell you, that older feller knew how to use them too, his hands a blur.'

Dave Tanning sat up a little straighter in his chair.

The old man took another sip of beer and wiped foam from his beard with a dirty sleeve. 'Saw him gun down three men in a showdown. Took one in the shoulder and could never use them guns again.'

'Is this Mitchell his son?' asked Dave Tanning.

'Nope. That Mitchell never married but he raised his nephew out in gold country. Treated him like a son though. Every night I heard the kid practicing with them old Colts. When his uncle died the youngster took over his stake and continued working with the Colts. Those who saw him said he was faster than his uncle.'

'Did he have any luck with the gold stake?' Tanning bought another beer and placed it in front of the old miner.

'Ha! Nothing but. Why he spent more time working than anybody I knew. He pocketed a huge bankroll aiming to raise cattle. He didn't want to spend the rest of his life digging for gold.'

'Ranching? Any idea where?'

'Nope, but now it appears he has his eye on some land in this area.'

The elder Tanning got up from the

table and bought the old miner another beer. Nugget pulled the beer close and smiled up at the wealthy rancher. The Tanning boys followed their father out of the bar and gathered outside the door.

Dave Tanning pointed to the general store down the street. 'Mitchell is picking up that strange package in the morning. Alan, Luke, I want you two to get on home and get some shuteye and follow him in the morning. I want to know where this land is that Mitchell is thinking of ranching.'

'Yes, Pa,' replied Luke and Alan together as they mounted their horses and rode toward the family ranch.

Will Tanning stepped in front of his father. 'Pa, Mitchell made me look bad in front of my girl! I want to go along with Luke and Alan. Heck, it's more my fight than theirs.'

Dave Tanning slowly lifted his head until his eyes locked with Will's. 'Boy, you listen good; we need cool heads for this. Your brothers can handle it.'

Will stormed out of the saloon and climbed onto his horse. He yanked on the reins and his horse turned north. The young rancher rode at full gallop toward the family ranch. Alan and Luke rested before attempting to discover where Mitchell planned to ranch.

2

The next morning brought sunshine and the promise of a fine day. Mitchell rose with the sun and packed his small bag. Through a crack in the curtains he surveyed Main Street. A wagon heading south from the livery stable provided the only activity on the street. Chet looked closer at the shadowed areas. Movement caught his eye in the darkness between Tanning's office and another building. Here he saw the outline of two horses. In Tanning's office people shuffled about. Mitchell expected the Tannings would keep an eye on him and they did not disappoint. Chet paid his hotel bill and walked into the dining room where he enjoyed a leisurely breakfast of ham and eggs. As he finished his third cup of coffee he saw the storekeeper open up shop. Mitchell tossed a coin on the table and exited the hotel.

He looked up at the sun and frowned. The curtains in Tanning's office closed as he crossed the street and entered the general store. The storekeeper looked up from the newspaper opened on his counter.

'Reckon you're here for your package.' he said.

'That's right and I'll take two of those large water sacks.'

'You heading out of town today? What direction?'

'Don't know for sure.' Chet gave the storekeeper money and left the store.

He carried the water sacks to the livery stable. Here he filled the sacks and his two canteens with fresh water. He draped blankets over the water sacks to keep them cool. The young boy helped him saddle his roan.

'Take this mule over to the general store and load on my supplies,' said Chet, handing the young man another coin.

'Yes, sir, right away.'

Mitchell eased himself into the saddle and rode slowly down Main Street to the general store where he tied his loaded mule to his horse. As he left the opposite end of town he looked over his shoulder and saw two of the Tanning boys running out of the office and into the dark alley. A grin spread across Chet's face. 'Time to have some fun.'

Mitchell headed across the grassland in the opposite direction to the Three Points and the hidden valley. He kept his hat over his eyes and his pace slow. The Tanning sons kept at a good distance so Chet knew they had been ordered by their father to follow him; not confront him.

After four hours of steady riding Chet arrived at an isolated small grove of trees. He removed the packs from the mule and the saddle from his horse and set them in the shade. It was fairly warm but not unbearably hot. Still, as the hours dragged by and with only small canteens of water, the Tanning brothers would feel the heat much more than would Mitchell. In the soil under the trees he dug two small holes and lined them with two pieces of leather he carried on the mule. He filled the leather bowls with water from the sacks and the two animals drank their fill.

He touched the top of the box and it pleased him that it was not overly hot. Mitchell threw a blanket over it and soaked it in cool water. As Chet drank from one of his large canteens he glanced over at the Tanning boys sitting under the midday sun at the crest of the small hill half a mile away. Only their heads peeked over the hill, keeping watch on Mitchell.

Alan and Luke drank from their half-empty canteens, sparing a little for the horses although they knew it wasn't enough for the big animals.

'Why didn't you bring an extra canteen?' asked Alan.

'Don't see one on your saddle either,' replied Luke.

The brothers squinted through the sunlight at Mitchell sitting in the shade of one of the trees.

'I wish we were a little closer,' said Luke. 'I'd put a bullet in him if we were.'

'We'd both like to do that but Pa made it clear we should find out what land he's after so we can beat him to it. Then we can get rid of Mitchell.'

Mitchell dozed comfortably in the shade knowing his horse would warn him if anybody approached. Two hours later he got to his feet and stretched. The brothers were pleased to see Mitchell saddle his horse and load the box and other purchases on the mule. Frustration rose again as Chet checked and rechecked the load. Finally, smiling at the intentional delay, Mitchell put foot to stirrup and lifted himself into the saddle.

Mitchell continued riding away from the Three Points, winding his way through the rolling land. He first expected the locals to think him crazy for attempting to ranch the hidden valley. After all, many had tried to access the lush land but all had failed; some had died trying. The trouble would come when they discovered his plan. A lot of trouble, mostly from the Tannings. After all, much of the water flowing through the area's ranches started at the Three Points and water equaled survival in these parts. Mitchell knew his cattle would use very little of the water but had no doubt Tanning would surely do everything he could to stop him and take the land for himself. What would the handful of smaller ranchers in the area think? Would they side with Tanning?

As sunset approached Chet rode straight to the center of a large valley of nearly open land. Again he found shelter under some trees while the Tanning brothers sat in the open with little or no water. He knew he was playing with fire as the boys might simply close in and shoot it out with him. Chet guessed right that Dave

Tanning ran the family with an iron fist and had told them only to follow him. He brewed some coffee and settled down for the night again with the horse there to warn of anyone approaching.

'I expect the Tanning boys have about had it,' said Chet to the roan as he saddled up early the next morning. 'Let's turn to the east and really confuse them.'

Chet turned to his right, riding directly into the sun. A mile or so later he reversed directions but rode at a slight angle away from Alan and Luke.

Their canteens now empty, the Tanning boys licked their cracked lips and shook their head at Mitchell.

'Is he searching for something?' Luke asked.

'I don't know. I suspect he's loco.'

'Maybe, but I think that he's trying to drive us loco or send us to an early grave if we don't get some water soon.'

Mitchell zigzagged for a few more hours then headed straight into the sun.

The brothers shook their heads and

followed Mitchell, baffled by the strange route.

'He's headed nowhere.' said Luke. 'He's just playing with us.'

'Luke,' said Alan, 'if I don't get a drink of water soon I'm going to keel over.'

'I've about had it too. Let's head back to the ranch. Word will reach us soon enough about where he's heading.'

Mitchell stopped at the top of a rise and watched the brothers ride off. He watched for twenty minutes, making sure they weren't trying to trick him and double back to get on his trail again. The brothers dipped behind a hill far into the east before Mitchell continued on his way. He skirted some sparse trees growing in rocky soil, soil that showed few prints. Here he stopped and poured more cool water on the blanket covering the box. He quenched his thirst and continued his journey.

The area was new to him. He made a

point of choosing different routes each time he rode to or left the Three Points. This path brought him to rough terrain, very dry and hilly. Here he slowed the pace as the horse and mule struggled on the rocky surface.

Two hills separated by a narrow path, a dried up creek bed, stood in front of Mitchell. The steep sides of the narrow path shot up fifteen feet. On the right the rock face continued up to the top of the hill at a forty-five degree angle. The left face of the path sat in shadow but Chet saw a small plateau fifteen feet above the creek bed. As he neared and fell into shadow from the other hill he saw that the plateau was actually the edge of a waterfall sitting dry until the next rainy season.

Even in shade the relentless heat made Chet wish the falls were running; riding through the falling water would have been refreshing.

The roan carried Chet under the waterfall lip at a slow pace, the mule trailing. Chet stopped as small pebbles rained down on him. He looked up just as a dark figure standing on the edge of the dry waterfall dropped a large rock directly over him. Chet moved his head to the side but the boulder still slammed into the back of his head. He tumbled off the roan and landed on the bed of stones. The last thing he saw before he blacked out was the man on the ledge, standing with his hands on his hips.

Mitchell's head throbbed as he regained consciousness. The heat of the sun pounded down on his bare head, compounding the pain from the gash where the rock had hit him. His lips were dried and cracked. He tried to lift his hand to block the sun but it would not move. In fact, both hands were tied to large boulders with rope. A pile of heavy rocks held his legs in place. His position, on a slight slope facing south, had total exposure to the sun. Chet saw the Three Points directly below the sun. He knew that was west and that meant he had been unconscious for over twelve hours.

A snicker caught Chet's attention. It

came from a tree twenty feet to his left, the only shade in the area. Someone sat against the tree. Mitchell squinted as he tried to make out the face.

'Wondering who outsmarted you?' The man stood up and walked out of the shadow. 'I bet you are.'

Chet didn't know for sure who it was, but recognized the short powerful build of a Tanning. He didn't have to wait long to get an answer. Will Tanning walked up to him, rifle in one hand, canteen in the other.

Will took a long pull on the canteen, letting water splash over his face and onto his clothes. 'Damn, that's fine. That water of yours is just what I needed. Now then, let's hear some of those funny things you said in front of my girl.' Will drove his boot into Chet's ribs. 'Aren't so talkative after a full day in the sun, are you? I frankly didn't know if you were going to wake up at all. Actually, I didn't much care.'

Chet's dry lips formed a smile. Will kicked Chet in the ribs again.

'Why don't I tell you what I've been up to while you've been resting in the heat?' Tanning waved his arm around in a circle. 'Why, after I tied you down I took my whip to your horse and mule. They hightailed it out of here, with your fancy guns in a saddle-bag. Now you're going to learn not to mess with a Tanning. I'm going to take your last canteen of water and head on home. I expect that by the time I get home and sit myself down at the dinner table the buzzards will be helping themselves to your sorry hide.'

Will Tanning walked over to the shade of the tree and climbed onto his horse. He rode up to Mitchell and smiled down. 'You should have stayed in the mines, Mitchell. You're no match for a Tanning.' Will laughed and rode away.

The hours moved slowly by. Mitchell's throat felt like sand and he lost feeling in his hands from the tight rope. He watched the sun glide gradually across the sky. When it passed midday he passed out.

3

A sharp pain in his left shoulder woke
Chet. Was it a coyote looking for a meal
or perhaps one of the buzzards
mentioned by Tanning? Chet tried to
open his burnt eyelids. With great pain
he managed to open them, only to find
himself in the shadow of a man. Had
Tanning decided to come back and
finish him off?

'Mister, can you hear me?' asked a
voice new to Mitchell.

The man knelt beside Chet and
poured water into his mouth, the finest
water Mitchell had ever tasted.

Chet's watched the man untie his
hands. He was a young man in his teens.
He helped Chet into a sitting position
and fed him more water. 'There you go,
Mr Mitchell.'

'Thanks.' Chet's voice was scratchy
and low. He studied the young man's

face but didn't recognize him.

'That's fine, stranger. My pa always told me to help.'

'My name is Mitchell, but you seem to know that already.'

'You're new, but already making a name for yourself. Word got to our ranch about you showing up the Tannings. My name's Jake Hart and we have a small spread just beneath the Three Points.'

Chet sat up and rubbed his sore wrists. 'Well, you tell your pa he can be proud of you. What brings you out here and how did you know my name?'

'I was hunting deer. I just got out here and first thing I come across is a stray horse and mule.' Jake pointed to Chet's roan and mule under the same trees where Will Tanning had sat. 'I backtracked them here. Papers in the saddle-bag had your name so I figured you weren't trouble.'

'Well, I hope I'm not. But I owe you and I promise to make it up to you some day.' Chet stood up and shook

Jake's hand. He then walked around to exercise his stiff legs.

'That's OK.' Jake looked at the sun. 'I'd best be heading back. My folks will worry. Why don't you come along and rest up at our house?'

'I'll be fine on my own and come by soon. I promise.'

'All right. You've plenty of water on the mule.' Jake Hart hung his canteen over the saddle horn and rode off toward the Three Points.

Chet climbed onto his roan and headed toward a grove of trees a mile north. At the end of the trees flowed a shallow creek that started on the Three Points. Mitchell rested here and washed his body in the cool water. He found his Colts in the saddle-bag and checked that they were loaded. He slipped the loaded pistols in his holsters and climbed back on his horse.

Despite his aching body he took advantage of the cool darkness and rode straight to the base of the Three Points. A short distance up the trail

Mitchell reached his usual rest area, a plateau overlooking the grassland. On one of his first trips up the trail he had discovered a small spring near the grassy plateau. When he had first seen the tiny trickle of water it ran down some flat rocks and disappeared into a small mossy crack. With a small mining pick he had chipped away at the rocks, creating two small troughs that gathered the water.

He wiped down and staked the horse and mule. A smile crossed his face at the thought of what the locals would say when he started the next phase of his plan. One thing was certain, everyone within many miles would know. Chet checked the box again and found it cool. He pulled out his bedroll and slept under the trees until first light.

The next morning Chet brewed coffee and moved some branches aside, exposing a path leading up the slope to the narrow passage in the rock wall between two of the mountains. With the heavy box on his shoulder he trudged up the path leading to the rock wall. Pain shot through his body as the box rubbed against his burnt shoulder. Chet squeezed behind a massive boulder and disappeared into the narrow crevice in the rock wall just wide enough for a man to pass. The only light in the narrow passage streamed down from the slender opening at the top that followed the winding route of the fissure. Even with the light Mitchell sometimes had to feel his way along the rocky corridor, at times crouching down to get past protruding rocks. The damp uneven ground made footing precarious. The slow walk took forty minutes, making Chet's shoulder ache with the weight of the heavy box. At last, a strip of light in the distance announced the end of the crevice.

A sea of green grass greeted Mitchell as he entered the hidden valley. Crystal blue water flowed in the river and creeks winding through the basin. The Three Points and cliffs in between made the area seem small but Mitchell had carefully measured the land and knew it would easily carry up to four thousand head of cattle. His dog, Dagger, barked and ran around Chet, welcoming him on his return to the valley.

With two more trips through the passage Mitchell had brought the rest of his supplies to the valley. He ate a hearty meal that night and dropped onto his bed, exhausted and sore, but content.

Chet had spent weeks constructing the cabin sitting on a knoll in a crescent of trees next to one of the three creeks winding through the valley like ribbons. The heavy trees to the north of the cabin would protect it from the harsh winds of winter.

The next morning, as Chet sipped hot coffee on the porch, a shadowed figure dashed behind the cabin. Mitchell grabbed his Colt and crouched behind a stump. Moments later Chet smiled and returned the gun to its holster as a healthy buck, one of the many deer in the valley, walked slowly out the other side of the cabin and sipped water from the creek. Mitchell and the deer shared the valley with rabbits, eagles, and many other animals.

In preparation for cattle arriving in the valley Chet had constructed three gated wooden bridges over the deep creeks that formed ideal barriers for separating the cattle. He had built fences in the few shallow areas to secure the enclosures. Smaller corrals near the barn and other fences would come later.

Near one of the other cliffs, between two of the Points, rested a large pile of freshly cut lumber. The flat wall of stone, far too steep even for a goat to climb, threw a long shadow over the lumber. This thirty-foot-high wall provided the key to Chet's plan to ranch in the valley.

★ ★ ★

The two horses carrying Luke and Alan Tanning hung their heads low as they trudged up to the small stream near the family ranch. The horses drank deeply, as did the two brothers.

Alan filled his hat with fresh water and dumped it over his head. 'I look forward to meeting that skunk Mitchell real soon. Why, he dang near killed us out there.'

'He's a sly one, that's for sure,' replied Luke as he joined Alan and the horses under some trees.

The two brothers rested out of the sun for an hour and then climbed back on their tired horses and rode toward the family ranch, both wondering how they would explain things to their father. Two ranch hands looked in amazement at the weary, dirty horses as they took them from Alan and Luke. The boys walked up to the large log ranch-house and found their father sitting on the veranda, smoking a cigar.

'Well, boys,' said Dave Tanning as he

took a puff on the cigar, 'what's that Mitchell fellow up to?'

'Can't say for sure, Pa. He gave us the slip,' lied Alan, not wanting to tell his father that they gave up after only two days because Mitchell had played them for fools.

'He what?' The elder Tanning sat up straight in his chair.

'Yeah,' added Luke. 'He's slick, mighty slick.'

'I see.' Dave Tanning knew his boys weren't experienced trackers and let it go. His claim on his land was solid but it wouldn't be the first time someone had tried to steal someone else's land. 'All right, you two get yourselves cleaned up and have Cookie fix you some food.'

'OK, Pa,' said Luke.

The boys disappeared into the ranch house. Their father leaned on the railing of the veranda, surveying his land bathed in moonlight. Will rode up with a wide smile on his face.

'Well Pa, I looked after that coyote

Mitchell.' Will climbed off his horse and tied it to a rail.

'How so?'

'I followed Alan and Luke at a distance and continued on when they couldn't. I knocked Mitchell off his horse and left him tied up under the hot sun. Heck, a better man than him would already be dead.'

Dave Tanning nodded. 'Where'd this happen?'

'Beside those two hills where we kept that small herd last spring.'

'Very well. Go join your brothers and get something in your stomach. It's getting late.'

Will walked into the house and hung his hat beside the door. Dave Tanning followed him into the house but walked into his office and sat behind his desk deep in thought.

The following afternoon Dave Tanning had one of the hands saddle his fastest horse. He climbed into the saddle and headed straight to the hills Will had mentioned. As he neared the hills he scanned the horizon and saw a lone rider pulling a pack animal at a slow pace. He couldn't make out who it was at the distance but had a good idea it was Mitchell. Tanning had learned how to track in his youth and easily found the start of the trail of the rider he had seen. He got off his horse and inspected the ground. He saw where Mitchell had been tied. On top of the tracks from Mitchell's two animals he recognized prints from Will's horse. Near the same trees another set of tracks had led Mitchell's horse and mule back. The boot prints of the unknown rider showed that he had untied Mitchell.

Dave Tanning climbed back on his horse and rode home. He took his sons into his office and told them what he had discovered.

Will threw the glass he was holding into the fireplace where it shattered. 'Damn, I had him and he got away.'

Will grabbed a bottle of whiskey and a fresh glass. He went and sat outside on the veranda and drank half the bottle. The next day Will saddled his horse and led it out of the barn. He decided that the time had come to speak to Lisa Cullen. She had forgiven him in the past for things he had done. Will tried to fight off the uncomfortable feeling building in him about how things were with Lisa. Was it that she had been growing more and more mature and self-confident over the last few months? Was it that he had begun taking her for granted? Or was it the arrival of that new fellow Mitchell? Whatever the cause, Will had the bull-headedness of a Tanning and was used to getting things his way.

He climbed onto his bay and pointed it directly at the small Cullen ranch. It was a short ride to Lisa's home, which sat on the edge of the Tanning spread, about halfway to the Three Points. Will grew more and more uneasy as he approached the small house sur-rounded by corrals. The grounds were clean and orderly, as Lisa's father, Steve

Cullen, took pride in his small piece of land and buildings.

Steve Cullen sat on a heavy wooden chair on the porch in front of his cabin. He studied the approaching rider from quite a distance. The direction suggested the rider was from the Tanning ranch and Cullen expected it was Will. Cullen had tolerated Lisa's interest in Will despite the Tanning family's history of bullying its neighbors. Now that Lisa had seen the real character of the young man, she was deeply upset. Lisa had spent the last few days alone in the small meadow near the house, thinking about her life. She had refused to discuss the incident that had caused the bruising on her arm with either her father or her mother, Susan. The constant pressure Cullen had been under to sell his ranch to the Tannings had eased when Will and Lisa had started seeing each other. If Lisa broke off with Will, it would rekindle the pressure to sell and the animosity would make it even worse. Steve and his wife liked their life here and dreaded receiving more pressure to sell and leave.

The door to the house creaked open and Susan and Lisa joined Steve on the porch. They watched the rider approach.

'It's Will,' whispered Lisa solemnly.

'I think it's best that you two go back in the house,' said Steve. 'I don't see any good coming out of this.'

Lisa calmly turned to face her father. 'No, Pa, I can handle it. You know that Will has a temper and is fast with a gun.'

Steve shook his head. 'No, I can't let him hurt my kin. It just isn't right.'

Steve reached into the shadow to his left, picked up his rifle and placed it on his lap.

Steve's eyes never left the approaching rider. 'Now Susan, you get Lisa into the house and lock the door.'

Susan wrapped her arm around her daughter and guided her into the house. Lisa took one last look at her father as the door closed. Steve heard the wooden bar slide across its supports, securing the door.

Young Will Tanning rode up fast, pulling the reins hard to stop his horse just shy of the modest house. He wore clean clothes and polished boots. As usual, his guns were tied down. Steve Cullen hated seeing animals abused and Will's treatment of his horse confirmed his dislike of the man.

'Afternoon, Steve.' Will straightened his hat and roughly turned his horse to the left so he faced Cullen squarely. 'Got ourselves another warm day.'

'Suppose so.' Cullen's eyes never left Tanning.

Will locked eyes with the older man. 'I rode over to talk to Lisa.'

Steve leaned back in his chair, allowing Will to see the gun resting on his lap. 'Afraid that won't be possible. You best turn your horse around and head back home.'

'Might want to reconsider that, old man.' Will moved his hand off the saddle horn and let it hang near his gun. A wry smile crossed Tanning's face. 'You know that we Tannings tend to get our way.'

'Maybe.' Cullen suddenly swung his rifle up and had it pointed at Will before the younger man had a chance to move. 'But I don't take kindly to threats, boy.'

Will sat there stunned. He knew Cullen knew how to raise cattle. He never guessed the quiet man knew how to handle a weapon. He stared down the dark barrel which was pointed at him.

'Why, that isn't being a good neighbor, Steve.' Will slowly lifted his right hand and scratched his chin.

'Neither is coming onto someone else's land and making demands.'

'Don't expect this'll be your land much longer.'

'That so? Are you the one that's going to take it away from me?'

'Not today, Cullen. Not today. But I promise you that the Tannings are in the habit of teaching lessons.' Will's face grew tight with anger.

Steve Cullen pointed his rifle in the direction of the Tanning ranch. 'You boys and your pa have made things about as bad as possible for us small ranchers. Now I'll only tell you this once. Get off my land and stay off. You're no longer welcome here.'

Will noticed the rifle pointed away from him, grabbed his gun, and brought it up. Cullen heard a roar and felt a sharp pain in his left shoulder. The barrel of Will's pistol spat smoke. Cullen's rifle fell to his side and his right hand gripped his bleeding shoulder.

Will returned his gun to its holster. 'You consider yourself lucky, Cullen. If I had the inkling I could've put that bullet between your sorry eyes.'

Will gripped the reins and rode up close to the porch, his words delivered between gritted teeth. 'I figure after this you have two choices: tell that pretty daughter of yours to start seeing me again. If not, I'll see to it that the Tannings take away this pathetic piece of land. Now you get Lisa thinking right.'

Will turned his horse around and galloped towards the family ranch.

From the small window facing the porch Lisa and her mother watched Will ride off. They threw off the board blocking the door and ran out onto the porch. They knelt beside Steve, Susan looking at the wound under the shirt.

'How bad is it, Ma?' asked Lisa.

'Not as bad as it looks.'

'It just nicked me,' said Steve. 'I must be getting slow in my old age. I don't know how I could have trusted that coyote for even a second.'

Steve Cullen had a powerful build developed from years of hard work keeping the ranch going. His spread rested close to the Three Points and never lacked water thanks to the river running between his land and that of the Tannings. The Cullens spent count-less hours clearing and working the soil closer to the Points, land capable of growing vegetables to sell in town to augment income from raising cattle. This made life more comfortable as the profits from raising cattle on such a small piece of land were meager. As the land dried out in the heat of summer the most they could hope to raise was eight hundred head.

Susan and Lisa helped Steve into the house where Susan dressed his flesh wound. 'Damn fool thing you did threatening a Tanning,' said Susan. 'Things are tough enough without having them causing us more trouble.'

Steve winced as he twisted his shoulder. 'I can look after myself and this family.'

Steve Cullen had grown up on a ranch in the north before moving with his new bride Susan to Tanning. In his younger days he commanded respect as a relentless foe in a fight and a crack shot with a rifle. This second talent helped provide meat for the young couple in the early days on the ranch through hunting.

Cullen pulled his wife close with his right arm and smiled. 'We have to deal with those Tannings eventually. If I have to take a bullet in the shoulder on the way, so be it.'

Susan leaned on her husband's good shoulder and her voice softened. 'I know, I know. You did what you had to do to keep that troublemaker away from our daughter.'

Lisa walked over and sat beside her father. 'I'm sorry I got involved with him, Pa. This is all my fault.'

'Don't believe that for one minute, Lisa,' replied Steve. 'Them Tannings are making life miserable for everyone in the area. We'll just keep our distance from them as best we can and deal with whatever comes up.'

Up in the hidden valley Mitchell walked to the cliff nearest his cabin and looked up the steep rocky face. Learning about the ancient passage into the valley had taken time but eventually he had sorted through the rumors from the locals and elderly Indians and discovered the crevice in the wall. The challenge of getting cattle to the lush grass had taken months of thinking, hiking, and climbing. He had never found an access any wider than the old passage. He had investigated most of the area inside and outside of the hidden valley and concluded that he would have to use his imagination to achieve his goal.

Many hours of contemplation had brought him to this moment, and the next step that would move him forward. This also included a literal step, a step up onto a board wedged into a small crack in the wall near his cabin. He lifted himself onto the board and gripped two rocks sticking out of the wall just over his head. He moved upwards on steps created by nature and others chipped out of the wall with his mining tools. The climb took twenty slow minutes but his last step onto a flat rock brought him within reach of the top of the cliff. He gripped the ledge and pulled himself up. Sweat poured off his brow and he wiped it dry with a bandanna as he stood looking over the grasslands pushing out to the horizon. The grass, while thick, would become dry as the summer wore on. He turned around and looked at the comparatively green grass of the high valley protected from much of the pounding sun by the mountains.

The idea of accessing the valley over the massive mountains was out of the question as they had sheer, jagged sides. Only the three cliffs between the mountains provided two possibilities, both of them tough. The first option, widening the passage in the thickest of the three cliffs, required years of backbreaking work chiseling away the solid rock walls. A trail up to the outside of the wall suitable for cattle only extended to the point where the roan and mule were hidden, the rest was too steep for access. The north wall's grade was even steeper and the wall higher and solid. The only possibility for getting cattle up to the wall and through it involved the cliff on which Mitchell stood.

The slope leading up to this cliff started as grassland on the edge of the Cullen ranch. Chet had walked the route to the edge of the cliff many times. He had found four obstacles of varying difficulty preventing cattle reaching the valley from this direction, the same obstacles that prevented Tanning or others from claiming the valley. The grassland quickly became heavy sloping forest that was passable for cattle, but only if cleared. Mitchell had cut his way through on his first hike with a razor-sharp knife and an axe. The exhausting trek had taken two days. Mitchell had slept well despite the sore shoulders and blistered hands developed on the hike.

This had brought him to the second challenge: a deep gorge. The roar of the pounding river had grown in intensity as he had worked his way up the gradual slope. The noise level had reached near deafening levels as he took the final steps that brought him to the edge of the gorge. He had then pulled a red bandanna out of his pocket and tied it to a long branch, which he had cut off a tree. He had wedged the base of the branch under a large boulder and leaned it over another tree branch so that it stuck out a good distance over the gorge and was visible from a distance.

The river rushed by forty feet below, mists rising nearly halfway up the rocky sides. Mitchell had had to return to the edge of the Cullen land and cross the river in order to hike through the heavy trees and brush on the opposite side of the gorge. As he investigated the route from that point on the gorge to the cliff, a plan had started to form in his mind. A few days' rest prepared him for a grueling two days' hike, which duplicated the opposite side of the gorge in difficulty. He had found the land grew gradually steeper and created three cutbacks to get up to the river gorge. The trail to that point on that side of the gorge was impassable for cattle and horses. Again he had found himself beside the deafening river; the red bandanna fluttering in the wind like a flag.

He had made a small fire and brewed coffee, sipping the strong drink as he watched the water crash down the river while eagles glided by overhead. His focus had returned to the hike and he once again moved uphill, this time through thinner trees at the higher altitude. The terrain remained at a constant angle and the thinning trees allowed an easier visual inspection. His experience in reaching isolated gold mines in the California mountains aided him in calculating angles and finding a route suitable for cattle. He started the hike by following the gorge upwards for fifty yards. From here four natural paths joined by three cutbacks brought him to the two remaining obstacles to getting cattle into the valley: the towering cliff itself, and a narrow, deep valley at the foot of the wall.

Now he proudly stood on top of the rock wall, surveying what he had done on the trail on the outside of the wall in the months since he had taken that hike. The view that morning brought energy to Chet despite the many months of heavy, lonely work. The end of the task was at hand. His glance swept over the sprawling Tanning ranch and those of the smaller ranchers, including the Cullens. His thoughts turned to Lisa, whom he had thought of often while working on the trail. The sun splashed down on the rangeland filled with feeding cattle, making Chet once again dream of his own ranch.

The forest between the rangeland and the far side of the river gorge was a blend of light and dark green interspersed with grey rocks, and only a view from that high vantage point showed the subtle signs of the trail he had cleared to the edge of the gorge. The twelve-foot-wide trail's thick, forested sides created a natural fence. Logs from clearing the path filled in the thin areas in the trees where cattle might wander. Many weeks had passed before

Chet had reached the bandanna over the gorge, a usable trail in his wake.

The mist-filled gorge above the raging river required crossing, and by the time Chet had cleared the trees from the path to the edge, he had gained great skill with an axe. Plenty of tall trees lined the gorge. The trick was to fell the trees so they reached across the gorge, giving access to the other side. Twelve thick trees, six on each side, remained standing after the completion of the trail. Mitchell knew he had only one chance with each, as moving an eighty-foot-long tree was far beyond the abilities of one man.

He had chopped away carefully at the first tree, the one closest to the edge of the gorge. Most of the cutting occurred on the side of the tree facing the gorge and Chet had listened carefully over the sound of the raging river for the splintering wood as it started to fall. The faint snap of wood fibers signaled for Mitchell to clear the way. He backed off and stood twenty feet away as the huge tree slowly, very slowly, leaned over. It picked up speed as it fell and smashed onto the ground on the other side of the gorge with a heavy thump, slightly buffered by the dark green branches.

Chet had smiled contentedly at the first span of wood and hardly rested before chopping away at the second tree. It fell nearly parallel to the first, only slightly wider at the narrow top of the trees. The remaining usable tree on that side of the river had landed perfectly as well. Chet then trimmed branches and laid down cross-boards as he worked his way across the span. Once on the other side he had removed the cross boards and cut down two of the three trees. They also had fallen beside the first three trunks in an ideal position. The last tree had fallen across the other five at an angle. The first five trees had provided plenty of support, so Mitchell cut this one into lengths to form the frame of the railing on each side. With the deck boards nailed permanently in place, the railings had been the last sections needed. He had built them over five feet high and strong enough to withstand the pressure of the cattle pressing against them when herded across the bridge.

Several weeks later Mitchell had completed the bridge and cleared the trail from the opposite end of the river gorge to the edge of the ravine beside the rock wall. This path had zigzagged on the steeper terrain and required fencing along the edge of the trail. With spans of thinner logs spaced between stout trees along the trail he had built a fence easily capable of keeping the cattle and riders safe.

The bottom of the trail remained blocked by twelve feet of heavy forest to prevent discovery of the trail before he could complete it. What would people think? Would they be angry at sharing the water? Would they take up arms? Mitchell had given this plenty of thought and would deal with it soon. Two more challenges awaited the former miner, the ravine outside the wall and the wall itself.

He breathed the fresh air and turned to face the valley. The next few days he rested outside his cabin, imagining cattle grazing on the rich green grass in front of him.

A few days later, bright sun greeted Mitchell as he walked out of his cabin and stretched. A deer drinking at the creek looked back over its shoulder and bolted into a nearby grove of trees. Morning dew still covered the railing surrounding the porch of his cabin as steam rose from the tin cup of coffee resting on it. The chair, under the cover of the veranda and protected from the dew, coaxed Chet to sit as he enjoyed his final cup of coffee before starting the next part of his plan.

He had liked to work alone in the gold mines but now he looked forward to having people around. He also knew that his actions would affect others and he might need help. The coffee finished, Chet cleaned the cup, returned it to the shelf and grabbed his hat from the hook behind the door. Now he would find out how the smaller ranchers would feel about a ranch in the valley.

4

The trip out through the passage proved much easier without the heavy box of supplies on his shoulder and he soon found himself welcomed by his restless roan, anxious to move. The mule, content with the nearby feed and water, paid Chet little attention.

Mitchell bridled and saddled his roan. The journey down the hill started slowly. He led the horse through the steep, winding path. Once on the gradual slope on the lower part of the hill he mounted the horse and made better time. Near the bottom of the hill he pulled back on the reins and stopped the horse. He took a drink of water from his canteen and gave his plan a final thought.

He nodded to himself and patted the neck of the horse. 'It's time.'

The horse broke into a canter across the rangeland. Soon Chet saw his destination: the Cullen house and barn sitting quietly in a grove of trees. A small wisp of smoke rose from the chimney. Lunchtime neared and they had likely started cooking food.

As Mitchell neared the house he noticed a curtain rustle slightly. He kept his hands in sight and rode slowly to the front of the house. The buildings and fences were modest but well maintained and organized, showing pride of ownership.

The roan instinctively walked toward the trough sitting in the shade of a wooden overhang in front of the house. The door opened, but Chet kept his back to it as he wiped down his horse. When thirty seconds went by with nothing said, he slowly turned around.

Lisa stood at the top of the three steps leading onto the small porch, her head in shadow from the porch roof. Mitchell stepped closer and her face came into view. Clearly she had been crying. Dried blood near a chair concerned Chet and he quickly looked around the yard. He checked the position of his Colts as he climbed the stairs and stood beside Lisa.

'Are you hurt, Lisa?'

'No,' Lisa replied. 'It's Pa. He's been shot.'

'How is he?'

'He'll be fine. It's in his shoulder. Will Tanning came here and Pa wouldn't let him see me. After he shot Pa, Will threatened to take our land.'

Chet nodded. 'Lisa, can your Pa talk? I may have a solution, a solution that will surprise you all and put an end to the Tannings trying to take over the whole area.'

'Yes,' replied Lisa. 'Pa can talk. The wound is minor. Let's go inside and I'll introduce you to my folks.'

'I'd like that.'

Lisa turned toward the door of the house. 'Pa's resting inside. I told him how you confronted Will. I think he'd be willing to talk to you, specially if it leads to getting the Tannings away from us.'

Mitchell stopped halfway to the door. 'Lisa, one way or the other I'm going to have to deal with the Tannings. I expect it would go better with others helping, but I can't say it will be easy.'

'I know. They're a stubborn bunch.'

Lisa opened the door and led Mitchell into the ranch-house. The furnishings were sparse but clean. The large stove dominated the room. To its left a table with four chairs sat near the wall. Cupboards with dishes and food lined the wall shared by the stove. Near a window overlooking the porch sat a man, with a bandage on his left shoulder. Sitting beside him was a woman wearing a worn dress and an apron.

'Chet Mitchell, this is my Pa, Steve Cullen, and my mother, Susan.'

Mitchell tipped his hat to Susan Cullen and shook hands with Steve Cullen. 'I'm pleased to meet you. I imagine Lisa told you that we met a while back in town.'

'Yes, she did,' nodded Steve. 'I'd like

to thank you for watching out for her.'

'Why don't you join us for a meal, Mr Mitchell? It's about ready,' asked Susan.

'Why that sounds just fine. It's been quite a while since I had a home-cooked meal. And please call me Chet.'

Chet noticed that Steve Cullen used both arms to get out of the chair by the window and walked with confidence to the table.

'You look none the worse with a bullet wound in the shoulder,' said Chet as he sat down across from Steve.

'Why, I've had worse wounds from a barbed-wire fence scratch.'

'Glad to hear it, neighbor.'

All three Cullens looked up at Mitchell before returning to their food. They had not heard of any land sales in the area.

Chet smiled. 'Perhaps we can discuss a business proposal that would be of benefit to all of us after this fine meal.'

Steve Cullen studied Mitchell for a few seconds. 'Might at that.'

The steaks, thick, rare, and juicy, cut easily.

'This is the finest meal I've ever had, Susan.'

Susan handed Chet a bowl of potatoes. 'Please help yourself.'

'Don't mind if I do.'

The Cullens talked of weather and horses but avoided the subject of where Mitchell would be ranching. Susan brought two chairs from the house out to the porch and they all sat in the shade, a slight breeze telling them that good things might be coming in their direction.

Steve reached inside the door and grabbed his rifle. 'I may have a bit of a sore shoulder but I can still hit one of those Tannings before they get anywhere near the house. From now on I have to keep this close; things are getting worse.'

Chet accepted a cigar from Steve. He struck a match on the railing and lit both smokes.

'Now, why don't we talk about this

business proposal, Chet?' Steve blew smoke into the blue sky.

'Fair enough,' replied Chet.

Chet reached over and put a hand on a small table against the railing and looked at Susan. 'May I?'

'Of course.' Said Susan.

Chet moved the table between them and pulled out a hand-drawn map. He spread it out on the table and rested his coffee on the windward side. The map showed the ranches in the area of the Three Points. The Tanning spread dominated the paper but Chet had clearly marked the other ranches. The names of the ranch owners appeared on their land. The Cullens noticed that Mitchell's name did not show on the paper.

Chet pointed at the center of the Tanning land. 'We all know that it's tough for the small ranchers against aggressive, large landowners like the Tannings.'

'Ain't that the truth,' nodded Steve.

'I'm proposing that we work together.

We should be able to raise large herds, with lots of weight.'

Lisa leaned forward. 'Chet, I can't help but notice that I don't see your name on a piece of land. Did you buy out one of our neighbors?'

'No Lisa, I have land, albeit a small piece compared to Tanning, but I still hope to raise cattle on it.' Chet leaned back on his chair, the cigar in his mouth. 'I've asked around and the word is you're honest people. So, I'm about to tell you about what I've been working on for the past several months.'

'Pretty much everyone in the area is wondering what you're up to.' Steve Cullen smiled. 'I confess we're mighty curious also.'

Chet pointed at the area between the Three Points.

Susan and Lisa's jaws dropped. Steve shook his head.

Steve looked Chet straight in the eye, reading him carefully. 'You're saying you found a way to ranch the hidden valley?'

'That's exactly what I'm saying.' Mitchell relayed what he had done over the last few months in preparation for the arrival of the cattle.

Steve looked over his right shoulder at the Three Points. 'Why, I can see the path you cleared, but just. You did a great job making it difficult to see, even from this distance.'

'That was the plan. I knew I only needed a few uninterrupted weeks to complete the trail. With your help we can have the job done in less than a week or ten days and cattle grazing within two weeks on the valley.'

The Cullens listened with amazement as Mitchell explained the plan for completing the trail.

Mitchell fell silent as the Cullens went into the house to talk things over. Minutes later they walked out together.

'It's a deal,' said Steve Cullen, and he shook hands with his new partner.

Two days later the three Tanning boys sat on their horses overlooking a herd of a thousand cows cropping grass on the part of the ranch opposite the Points. All three heads turned as their father rode up on his black. He briefly sat and studied the cattle.

The elder Tanning pointed to the west. 'Have the hands move this herd over to the greener grass in the trees, and you three give them a hand.'

Luke glared at his father. 'What? You know we just watch over the men.'

'Yeah,' added Will. 'We don't do no punching.'

'You'll do what I say and keep your mouth shut,' said Dave Tanning. Then he spat on the ground and rode away.

'What's with Pa?' asked Alan.

'Ah, he's just wondering about that Mitchell fellow,' replied Luke. 'He doesn't even know if he's still in the area.'

Will spun his horse around to face his brothers. 'Oh, he's around. I can smell that skunk. I just don't know where. But when I do see him lead will fly.'

The brothers grumbled amongst themselves before grudgingly joining the ten other men and moving the cattle to the sheltered grass.

The last of the herd was moved under the trees. The heat of September had dried much of the grass but the Tannings had more woodland with the grass protected from the sun than the other ranchers in the area.

Alan lifted up his canteen and took a long drink. Just as he took his last swallow the ground shook beneath him. Water spilled over his face and he wiped it off as Will rode up.

'Now what in blazes was that?' asked Will.

'Beats me,' replied Alan, grinning. 'Maybe that Mitchell fellow has taken to mining in the area.'

'Aw, there's no gold in these parts,' said Will.

The brothers helped the hired hands move the few straggling cows into the shaded grass. An hour later they started back to the ranch. When they were halfway they spotted riders approaching. As they neared, they recognized the powerful shape of their father on a fresh horse and a ranch hand with three more horses in tow. Just before Dave Tanning came up to his sons another explosion shook the ground.

'Pa!' exclaimed Luke. 'Where's that coming from?'

Dave Tanning pointed over his shoulder at the Three Points, where a cloud of dust floated towards the few clouds in the sky.

'Do you think that it's that Mitchell fellow?' asked Will.

'It would explain that mysterious box he had delivered,' replied Dave Tanning.

'Dynamite?' Luke spat on the ground. 'Well, I'll be! It makes sense, since he worked in the mines out west.'

'You three grab those fresh horses and have a look,' said the elder Tanning. 'And be careful, you hear?'

'We'll keep our eyes open,' said Alan calmly. 'Let's go see what he's up to.'

The three Tanning boys climbed onto the horses and lit out towards the

Points. They splashed through the shallow, rocky creek and picked up the pace. They thundered across the grassland toward the Three Points.

★　★　★

High on the hill to the left of the cliff over the ravine, Chet and Steve watched the dust settle from the second explosion. The two men had stuffed twenty sticks of dynamite into a deep crack one-third of the way down the outside of the wall. Chet had lit the long fuse and climbed up the rope ladder and up the hill. His experience had taught him that the effect of the explosives extended far beyond the area around the dynamite. He had Lisa and Susan stay in the center of the hidden valley while he and Steve sat on a level area of the hill well away from possible falling rocks.

The impact of the explosion had violently shaken the ground under them. Steven Cullen had never felt such power and he gained extra respect for the explosives.

The first explosion had sent tons of rock from the wall tumbling into the ravine, nearly filling the crevice. Once the dust had settled the two friends saw a twenty-foot-wide gap in the wall, the ground a jagged sheet of rocks of various sizes.

Chet scratched his chin as he analyzed the site.

'I propose you make the first trip through the new passage, Chet.' said Steve.

'Obliged, Steve, but we have one more thing to deal with before anybody passes through there.' Chet pointed to the top of the passage on the opposite side from where they now stood.

A lip of rock stuck out eight or ten feet over the opening.

'We best set one more blast to get rid of that,' said Chet. 'I've seen overhangs like that fall on miners.'

'What's the plan?'

'I suspect there are plenty of curious

people wondering what we're up to, including the Tannings. We'd best deal with this quickly and then we can keep an eye out for anyone thinking of coming by and having a look.'

Steve threw a rope over the overhang and wrapped the other end around his waist. Knots tied in the rope every few feet aided Mitchell's grip as he climbed, carrying three sticks of dynamite in his holster. Chet reached the underside of the overhang and looked for a place to wedge the dynamite. He found an opening near the middle, deep and wide enough to hold the explosives. The dynamite fit snugly into the hole, the fuse dangling six feet down, providing plenty of time to get clear of the explosion.

Mitchell slid down the rope, stopping at the end of the fuse.

'Ready to run, Steve?' Chet joked, as he struck the match. The fuse hung near the rope and within easy reach. Chet reached out with the match and touched the fuse. It caught and sent out a cascade of sparks, hitting Chet squarely in the face. Mitchell dropped the match and instinctively grabbed for his eyes. His left hand lost its grip, sending the big man dropping. Still blinded, he grabbed the rope and his hands slid over two knots before he came to a stop ten feet from the ground.

The fuse continued to move towards the dynamite as Mitchell edged himself toward the rocky ground.

Steve stood below, keeping the rope taut. 'Five more feet, Chet. Nice and easy now.'

'How's the fuse?' asked Chet.

'About halfway. It'll be close.'

'I'm jumping, try to grab my arm.' Chet released the rope as he said the words, knowing time was everything.

He fell the five feet, landing to Steve's right. Chet's foot slipped on a smooth rock and sent him falling towards Steve.

'I have you,' said Steve, as he grabbed Chet's left arm and stopped him just short of falling on the jagged rocks.

'You best run, Steve. I'm still blinded and will slow you down.'

'Chet, I've got your arm. Just go as fast as you can in this direction. Step high, I'm leading you.'

'But — '

'No buts. Let's move.'

Steve held a tight grip on Chet's arm and pushed him toward a large boulder. Chet rubbed his eyes with his free hands as he stumbled over the loose rocks.

'To the left a bit,' yelled Steve, as Chet came up to the giant boulder.

Steve glanced up at the fuse and saw that it had inches to go to reach the explosives. He shoved Chet to the ground behind the boulder and fell on top of him.

The noise from the explosion pounded in their ears. As the overhang crashed to the ground it also spewed rocks, some as big as fists, shooting through the air, several flying directly at Chet and Steve.

5

The rocks sailed toward the two men and crashed into the top of the boulder. Smaller chunks bounced off the opposite side of the new passage and slammed into Steve's back.

The dust cloud, while smaller than the one from the first explosion, still blocked the view of Lisa and Susan. As the wind pushed it away like a drawn curtain they rushed toward the two men. Steve winced as he got to his feet and helped Chet lean against the boulder. Both men wore a layer of dust.

'Steve, Chet! Are you OK?' Susan asked, as they approached the two men.

Steve hugged his wife. 'I'm all right, just have a sore back from some flying rocks. Chet took some sparks in the eyes and can't see.'

Lisa wiped Chet's face with a handkerchief. 'It's me, Chet. Let me help you to the house and we'll have a look at your eyes.'

Chet sat back in the chair on the veranda of his house. Lisa wiped his eyes with warm water. His vision slowly cleared. First he saw a vague image of the rich blue sky framed by the roof of the veranda above and the mountains beneath. Next he saw the outline of Lisa growing in clarity. Soon her beautiful face was all he could see, all he wanted to see. The bright sunlight filtered through Lisa's golden hair.

'I'm going to have a look at that bruise on your pa's back, Lisa,' Susan said, as she walked into the cabin with a fresh pail of water.

'Right, Ma.' Lisa leaned over Chet, dabbing his eyes with a warm cloth.

As his vision fully cleared Lisa leaned close, dabbing gently at the last few pieces of dust. She pulled back and their eyes locked. She smiled broadly.

She pulled the soft cloth back from his face. 'Better?'

'Perfect,' replied Chet softly. 'Thank you.'

Lisa blushed and stood back. Susan and Steve walked over.

Chet looked straight at them. 'Vision is just fine. Only a little sore but I expect that will pass.'

Mitchell and the Cullens walked out to the new passage. Piles of rocks stretched for thirty feet out from the blast area.

Steve's jaw dropped. 'If that isn't the most amazing thing I've ever seen.'

Susan took Mitchell's arm. 'You did it, Chet!'

'It's open,' said Mitchell, 'but there's plenty of work left to do.'

'Heavy work, but that never hurt anyone.' Steve said, as they walked over the crumbled debris and stood on top of the rocks filling the ravine outside the wall. They looked out over the rangeland, the Cullen ranch in the distance.

Chet stood behind Lisa. 'I think we can have cattle up here within a week if the rains hold off. But — '

The three Cullens looked at Chet

with concerned looks on their faces.

Chet also appeared serious. 'I figure we can expect more than cattle finding their way into the valley. The Tannings will be some upset that this land is now accessible and that they don't own it.'

As Chet spoke those words the Tanning boys reached the halfway mark on their ride around the Three Points.

Chet turned to Lisa and Susan and pointed. 'Ladies, would you mind going onto that small plateau over the new passage to keep watch while Steve and I work on clearing this area?'

Susan and Lisa agreed and climbed onto the small plateau above and to the south of the new passage, keeping a lookout. Lisa spotted the three mounted men closing from the west.

'Ma, there are riders coming.'

Lisa stood beside her mother, under the cover of low branches of a large pine tree. 'Should we call Pa and Chet?' she asked.

'Only if the Tannings make a move towards us,' said Susan.

The Tanning boys stopped directly below the plateau and looked up at the new opening into the valley. They could not see Lisa and Susan watching them.

Alan took off his hat and wiped his brow. 'Well, would you look at that? Mitchell has blown a hole in the wall.'

'He's still crazy,' Will said. 'I told you he wasn't smart. How is he going to get cattle up there, with a rope? He'd have to throw them across those gorges. A fool, I say.'

'Maybe,' Luke said quietly. 'Maybe. Let's see if we can get in for a closer look.'

The three riders rode back and forth several times in front of the heavy trees but didn't spot the cleared route hidden behind part of the forest. They gathered again away from the trees and took another look up at the opening in the rock wall.

'No way in that I can see,' Alan said.

'We'd best get back.' Luke turned his horse around. 'Pa will want to hear about this right away.'

Alan and Will spun their mounts around as well and the brothers rode away at a full gallop.

'Looks like they gave up,' Susan said.

'I think so too. But they'll be back; we can be sure of that,' replied Lisa.

Susan remained on watch while Lisa hiked down and told her father and Chet about the unwelcome visitors.

'You're sure it was the Tannings?' asked Steve.

'For sure, Pa. No doubt about it.'

'Good work, Lisa,' added Chet. 'We can expect another visit from them soon.'

'Don't worry,' Lisa responded quickly. 'Ma and I will keep a close eye out over both entrances while you two finish the trail.'

'That's a big help, Lisa.' Chet smiled warmly.

Chet found it more and more difficult to keep his thoughts off Lisa. She seemed to fit in perfectly in the valley. Was she feeling the same way about him? She spent most of her free time with him, even helping him move rocks when her father's shoulder required rest. She showed surprising strength and a willingness to work hard.

The work progressed well. Extending the trail from the valley to the bridge across the gorge took shape as they first leveled the area from the hole in the wall to the start of the trail on the other side of the ravine.

★ ★ ★

Will, Alan, and Luke climbed off their tired horses. Dave Tanning had paced back and forth on the veranda for most of the day off and on, constantly watching the horizon in the direction of the Points. Ranch hands also read the looks of concern on the faces of the three brothers as they led the exhausted horses into the barn. The brothers then headed straight into the large ranch-house. Their shadows reflected on the curtains of their father's study window as they passed on their way to the door.

Dave Tanning heard the stampede of boots headed his way and put the papers he held down on the desk. He had not been able to concentrate on them. His mind kept sorting through the possibilities when dealing with a man like Mitchell.

The sons lined up in front of their father just as they had done when they were young. They knew their Pa didn't like surprises, especially when it came to his pride and joy, the Tanning ranch.

Dave Tanning maintained his best poker face and slowly looked up from the papers. He knew the news was even worse than he'd thought when he studied the faces of his boys. 'All right, let's have it.'

Alan stepped forward. 'Pa, someone blasted a huge hole in the north wall on the Three Points, a big hole.'

Dave Tanning frowned. 'Mitchell!'

'You sure?' asked Alan.

Dave Tanning's face went sour. 'Of course it's Mitchell. There's nobody else with his expertise with explosives.'

'Pa, according to the law it's not anybody's land until they settle it,' commented Luke.

Dave Tanning's hand slammed down on the desk. 'I don't care what the law says. I own most of the land around the Three Points and that means I own it too. Do you all understand.'

All three boys nodded agreement.

'Good!' Dave Tanning calmed down and poured himself a glass of whiskey. 'Now we have lots to do so let's concentrate on that.'

Luke slammed his hat against his side, sending up a cloud of dust. 'How is he going to get cattle up there anyway? Heck, a mountain goat would have trouble making it up those hills, let alone trying to cross the river and gorge on the way up.'

Alan walked up to the credenza and poured himself a drink. 'Maybe, Luke. But I figure he must have found a way. Why else would he blow a hole through the wall?'

Dave Tanning opened a desk drawer

and pulled out a cigar. He lit it slowly and got out of his chair. A stream of smoke trailed him as he walked over to the window, taking some time to compose himself and think. While his mind swirled from problem to problem it kept returning to the vital issue of water, the foundation of life and ranching. He knew the hidden valley could hold thousands of head of cattle — cattle using water he wanted for his operation.

Several cowhands rode past the ranch-house. Dave Tanning decided that although he had a few men who could handle themselves in a fight and a few with exceptional ability, he would bring in professional gumen. Not a man to work from a position of weakness, he decided he had to improve his odds before taking action.

The three sons stood silently, having learned years earlier not to disturb their father when he was mentally wrestling with a serious problem.

Dave Tanning walked confidently

back to his desk and dropped into his chair. Keys rattled as he pulled them out of his vest pocket. The smallest key slid easily into the lock on the lower right-hand drawer. The heavy drawer slid open, exposing several tall piles of cash. His powerful hand fell onto one of the stacks. Experienced fingers counted out the appropriate number of paper-wrapped bundles of one hundred dollars and he placed them on top of the desk.

From those piles Dave Tanning grabbed five stacks of money and tossed them at Will. 'Boy, here's your chance to make things right. You ride into town and hire some gunmen. Use that money. Take the men out to the hidden valley through the narrow path and make it clear to Mitchell that the valley belongs to the Tannings. It did before and it always will.'

Will tucked the money in his pocket. 'My pleasure, Pa. I have a score to settle with Mitchell.'

Dave Tanning puffed on the cigar

hanging from the side of his mouth. 'If trouble starts, make sure those gunmen earn their pay. We don't want anything to happen to you. Understand?'

'Yes, Pa. I won't let you down.'

Will walked out of the office and left the house. A ranch hand walked past.

'Don,' said Will, 'I'm catching a couple of hours' shut-eye. Have a fresh horse ready for me then.'

The ranch hand waved. 'It'll be ready, boss.'

Will slept for two hours and then drank two cups of coffee. The bundles of cash rested securely in his pocket as he entered the barn. Don tightened the cinch on the bay and handed the reins to Will, who mounted the horse and checked the action on his rifle. He slid it into the hand-tooled scabbard on his saddle. Don opened the gate and Will guided the horse onto the worn trail leading to the town of Tanning.

Will pushed the horse and made it to town in forty-five minutes. He walked the horse past his usual saloon and didn't stop until he came to the rough Cullimore's Saloon at the far end of town. Will passed slowly, looking through the dirty windows. He was happy to see a good-sized crowd, including plenty of gunmen. Will tied his horse to the railing alongside several other horses and climbed the chipped stairs toward the bright light and noise flooding from the saloon.

He entered the bar-room that smelled of stale beer and smoke. The two poker games came to a halt and every set of eyes in the room fell upon him. The whispering men recognized him immediately and knew that Tannings didn't enter the Cullimore for the taste of the whiskey. Will walked straight to the bar and leaned an elbow on the polished brass rail surrounding the beer-stained wood. The poker games quietly restarted.

'A round on me, bartender.' Will dropped money on the bar. 'Make it a whiskey for me.'

Will took a sip from the low-grade drink and suppressed a wince. He held the drink in his left hand and turned to survey the crowd. Most of the men had dirt from the trail on their clothes. A few saluted him with their free drink, perhaps a hint that they could use some work.

The poker players returned to concentrate on their game and their piles of chips. The games at the Cullimore seldom followed the rules. One tall skinny man at the far table wore a smile as big as his stack of chips. He sipped the free drink and threw down his third full house in four hands. As he pulled the healthy pile of chips toward him, the barrel-chested man across from him spat into a cuspidor.

The heavy man leaned forward and glared at the skinny man stacking his winnings. 'I've been playing cards for fifteen years and I've never seen the likes of it, stranger.'

'Just a run of luck, fella. Why don't you let me buy you a drink?' The skinny man grinned and finished placing the last chip on the stack.

'Nobody's that lucky. You hear me?'

The people behind each man and the others at the table backed away.

'Just deal the cards. Your luck is bound to change,' said the skinny man.

'I can't deal without any chips.' The big man jumped to his feet and reached for his gun.

The big man's hand had barely gripped the handle of his gun when the skinny man fired twice under the table, hitting the bigger man in the left knee. The acrid smell of gunpowder filled the room. The heavy man fell backwards over his chair and crashed onto the floor. A man walked up and helped the wounded man limp out the door, leaving a trail of blood on the dusty floor. The other players at the table gathered their few chips and walked slowly away.

The thin man returned his gun to its holster and shuffled the cards, the huge grin still on his face. It was a fearless grin. 'Come on now, there are chairs free at the table. Who's up for a game?'

Will noticed that the slim gambler never bothered to glance around the room full of cut-throats to see if a friend of the shot man might seek revenge. Then Will saw why. Three men stood at the opposite end of the bar with their backs to the bartender, their hands hanging down near their tied-down guns. The skinny man looked up at his friends and his smile grew even wider and he threw his hands up in a sign of mock bewilderment. These men had his back.

The tall, thin man cashed out his chips and slipped the wad of bills into his pocket. He wandered over to the far end of the bar and talked with his friends. They all looked confident, tough, and gun-savvy.

'Bartender,' said Will quietly. 'Send four drinks over to that tall fellow and his friends.'

The bartender nodded and grabbed a dirty bottle from behind him.

'No.' Will pointed under the bar. 'The good stuff.'

'Right.' The bartender reached under the bar and pulled out an expensive bottle of whiskey, full and unopened.

He walked over to the four men and held up the bottle. The four men smiled and waved at Will. The slim man drained the smooth drink in one gulp and talked to his friends for a minute. Then he walked over to Will and offered his hand. 'Obliged. That's fine whiskey, Tanning.'

Will shook the man's hand and nodded at the bartender, who refilled his glass and those of the four men. 'It's that. And you're right, I am a Tanning, Will Tanning. Don't believe we've met before.'

'True.' The thin man's enormous smile remained in place. 'We make a point of learning the names of important people when we ride into a new town. The Tanning name was it in Tanning. The name's Frank McCall.'

'Just passing through?'

'Maybe, but we're always looking for work.'

'Well, I'm here looking for a few men to hire for a couple days. Pay's good but the work requires men who aren't afraid to use a gun if the need arises.'

'Why don't we refill this glass and talk about it?'

'Leave the bottle,' Will told the bartender as he poured whiskey into McCall's glass.

Will liked the nerve of the man, and sensed he and his friends would do almost anything for the right money. This was critical, as he didn't know what waited for them up in the hidden valley.

'Well, let's see if we're interested.' McCall waved at his friends. 'Come on over here, boys.'

McCall's three friends picked up their glasses and walked to the other end of the bar. Will noticed that their jovial demeanor didn't stop them from taking regular glances around the room, watching out for trouble.

'Will Tanning here has a job for us. Meet Sam Truman, Billy Presson, and Lead Walker.'

Will shook their hands. Truman had alert eyes and a trim build. Presson carried plenty of weight and all of it muscle. His face wore a much more serious look than his light-hearted companions. Lead Walker, short and slim, carried his guns low and had a confident swagger in his step.

'Lead, that's an interesting name,' said Will.

A grimace crossed Lead Walker's face and he tapped the bullets hanging on his belt. 'That's cuz I let my lead do my talking.'

The four men in front of Will stood in silence for a moment, then burst out laughing.

'Heck, my pa meant to name me Ted,' said Walker, 'but he was so drunk when he filled out the official papers they thought it said Lead and it was too late to change.'

'Now, what's the job?' asked Truman.

'Very well. There's a man fixing to ranch some land that my father says is ours. We want him gone,' replied Will.

'Simple as that.'

'Is it your pa's land?' asked Truman as he refilled the glasses.

'Don't matter. If Dave Tanning says it's his land, it's his land.'

'This land thief got a name?' asked Presson.

'Goes by the name of Chet Mitchell.' Truman leaned close to his friends but spoke loud enough for Will to hear. 'Heard of him. He has quite a reputation out west in the mining camps. Could be tough.'

Will got the message. 'We'll pay you very well.'

'What's well?' asked Presson.

'Five hundred each when the job's done.'

'I think we can do business.' McCall drained his drink. 'But we'll need five hundred up front ... supplies and such.'

'We'll supply everything you need.'

'Still, this sort of business don't involve a whole lot of trust.'

Will reached in his pocket and set

five hundred dollars on the bar. McCall picked it up and put it in his pocket.

'Why, I think we have a deal. How about another bottle of this stuff.' Presson slapped Will on the back and laughed. 'After all, we're partners now.'

Will bought another bottle and sat at a table in the corner while the four men celebrated their new job. The men stood about at the bar and drained the bottle before joining Will at his table.

McCall, the leader of the group, slammed a hand down on the table, his light-hearted demeanor hardened by whiskey. 'So, when do we leave, Tanning?'

'First thing in the morning; and be ready to climb a bit. Mitchell is holed up in a valley tucked up in the Three Points.'

6

At the Three Points the work progressed on the new trail through the
wall. Steve and Chet smashed and
carried rocks to the ravine and filled the
low areas. Working from left to right
they first rolled in large rocks, then
filled in between with smaller rocks.
Once close to level they shoveled on
gravel and dirt to create a smooth
surface. Halfway through moving the
rocks into the ravine they found a
boulder half the size of the cabin
hidden under smaller rocks.

Sweat poured off Chet's brow. 'Glad
we have some extra dynamite. This
should be the last blasting. I think we
can move the rest by hand.'

'Any way to blast the rock over
the edge and into the open area of the
ravine in one shot? It would fill in
the right side nicely.'

'Sure.' Chet leaned down and inspected the bottom of the boulder opposite the ravine. 'If we dig down here about four feet and use three sticks of dynamite it should move it into the ravine.'

'I'll get to digging.'

'No, Steve, you rest that shoulder of yours. By the time you get back with the explosives I should have the hole dug.'

Chet took a long pull of water from his canteen and set to work. He cleared the loose rocks behind the boulder. He grabbed a pick resting against the edge of the opening and walked up to the boulder. The first swing smashed the surface rocks, sending small pieces flying through the air. The next swing pushed deep, over one foot into the earth. He neared the appropriate depth and switched from the large pick to a small one he carried on his belt.

The hole was tight but he reached down and chipped away, gauging the width carefully so the explosives would fit in tight and the blast would focus on sending the boulder sailing into the ravine. Steve walked up with the sticks of dynamite and handed them to Chet. The three cigar-shaped sticks fit firmly into the hole, the fuse at the ready.

'Here goes.' Chet lit the fuse and jogged behind the inside of the rock wall beside Steve.

The blast shook the area. The force of the explosion pushed the giant boulder out of the hole and sent it crashing into the ravine.

Lisa walked up and waved away the dust in the air. 'Are you two disturbing the neighbors again?'

'Yup,' replied Chet. 'But that should be the last time.'

'Maybe another extra day's work filling the hole, but that beats taking a sledgehammer to that big boulder,' added Steve.

'I can help out here. Ma can see most of the approaches from the higher spot above the old passage,' offered Lisa.

'Thanks Lisa, but we need you sharing the lookout duties with your ma. Your pa and I can keep a good eye on this side while we work here. As far as I know these are the only two ways up here.'

Steve took a drink of water from his canteen. 'Legend talks about another way up, a very old and difficult way up that was abandoned when the passage was found.'

'Maybe, but I expect the trouble will come through the passage.'

'Want us to watch day and night, Chet?'

'No. I don't see anyone trying to make it up to the outside entrance during the night. It's too difficult to find in the dark in those thick trees. Besides, if we miss them and they get in the valley at night, Dagger here will let us know and I'll be sleeping nearby with rifle at hand.' Chet bent down and rubbed behind the ears of his dog. Lisa went back to the lookout, giving her mother a chance to go get some food from the cabin. Susan came up with a basket of lunch and she, Steve and Chet sat on the plateau above the passage, eating beef and homemade bread.

Steve Cullen chewed on a piece of bread. 'I best carry more rifle ammo. I expect it won't be long before we get a visit from the Tannings. Probably tomorrow.'

'I agree.' Chet nodded as he sipped hot coffee. 'Susan, we need you and Lisa to continue keeping a sharp lookout over the old passage for trouble. Be sure to give us as much warning as possible.'

Chet stood up and stretched as he looked at the sun. 'We can get in several more hours' work on the entrance. Susan, can you get that ammo Steve mentioned and some more water for us and take some food to Lisa over the passage?'

'Sure can. I'll be back shortly.'

Over the next few hours Chet and Steve managed to level twenty feet more area outside the hole in the wall, as well as clear the remaining rubble from the fallen overhang.

No visitors tried to approach the Points that afternoon or evening.

Mitchell wanted to get a good night's sleep, as he expected something would likely happen the next day.

Steve Cullen took a final visit to the plateau over the passage as the sun set. From this vantage point and with field glasses he could see that his herd of cattle peacefully cropped grass on the land around his house, undisturbed. The bright red sunset filled the sky. He hoped it wasn't a sign of things to come.

Will Tanning and his four hired guns started from town early. Will had stayed the night in the apartment above the family office. He put the men up in the Cullimore Hotel. As soon as they were up, they mounted and rode out to the Tanning ranch. They drew looks of concern from a ranch hand who knew what hired guns had meant in the past: trouble and death. Dave Tanning had risen early and walked out onto the veranda of the house and leaned on the railing.

He preferred to fight his own battles,

and as he got older would buy a place rather than risk lives. He had hired gunmen twice in the past to coax ranchers in the area to sell or move out and reasoned that he should again, as Mitchell had already attacked his son. As his stature in the area had grown, so too had his desire to keep trouble at a distance. The few remaining smaller ranches in the area struggled to survive and Tanning believed in time they too would sell to him. Besides, the idea of someone ranching the hidden valley and using some of his water infuriated him.

Dave Tanning looked down at the scruffy but tough-looking gunmen as they rode up but didn't bother to introduce himself. 'Get yourselves over to the cookhouse and grab some grub.'

'I expect we'll be back for another meal tonight, Pa. This Mitchell is just one man,' Will said confidently.

Dave Tanning looked at his youngest son and nodded before turning around and vanishing into the ranch house.

Will ate steak and eggs with the gunmen. For the most part their light-hearted mood returned as they got more food in their stomachs and the effects of the heavy drinking of the previous night wore off. The exception, Presson, only ate a few pan-fried potatoes and sat staring into the distance.

McCall sipped coffee. 'What's got into you, Presson, we've had tougher jobs than this?'

'I got some thoughts' — Presson looked McCall straight in the eye — 'but I'm not sure you want to hear them.'

Everyone at the table stopped eating and listened carefully.

'Speak up,' McCall said.

Presson got up from his chair and walked over to a window and pointed west. 'My folks raised me until I was fourteen in the gold area out west in California. Two towns away a fella named Mitchell grew himself a reputation with a gun. Old Colts if I remember right — old Colts with eagles on the handles. He kept those eagles polished so they shined like the sun. A warning to beware. Could this be the same man, Tanning?'

'It's the same Mitchell, but we have him backed into a canyon and alone.'

'Heck,' added McCall, 'no one man is a match for us, not even this snake Mitchell.'

'I suppose you're right.' Presson's mood picked up.

'We're paying you well, it's five on one, and the time has come. Let's ride.' Will jumped out of his chair and opened the door.

Chet had given up his cabin to the Cullen family for the week or ten days needed to prepare the trail into the valley. The stars provided his ceiling as he slept next to the small creek a short walk from the cabin. As usual, he woke early, the stars still twinkling in the crystal-clear sky. He leaned back in his bedroll, the smell of wood smoke drifting over from the cabin.

But his mind was conflicted. He knew there was trouble coming from the Tannings. He also knew it would come soon. If trouble was coming from the stubborn Tannings he wanted to get it over with. As his dislike of the Tanning family grew, so his fondness for the Cullens grew, too. Like Chet, they were hard working, honest folk, and getting them mixed up in this concerned him. He had especially grown fond of Lisa. She seemed to like the valley as much as he liked having her there. Even the animals enjoyed her company, with the robins almost chirping hello to her in the mornings.

The smell of bacon cooking coaxed Mitchell out of his bedroll and onto his feet. He walked toward the cabin and the door opened as he prepared to take the first step onto the porch. Lisa walked out, her head down as she tied up her flaxen hair in the back. She checked the knot and stood up straight, finding herself staring straight into Chet's eyes.

'Good morning, Lisa.' Chet whispered awkwardly.

Lisa blushed and smiled. 'Good morning. Did you sleep well? Somehow it doesn't feel right us using your home.'

'Don't give it a thought. I sleep soundly under the stars.'

'Well, come on in out of the cool air. Ma has breakfast on the table. I was on my way to get you.'

'I must say it smells great.'

Susan came out the door holding two steaming cups of coffee and handed them to Chet and Lisa. 'Good morning, Chet. Here, this'll warm you up.'

'Obliged.'

'Best you come in now, Chet, before the food gets cold.'

'Don't have to ask twice,' Chet replied as he climbed the steps and walked into the house.

As the daylight blossomed Lisa took her place as lookout over the thin passage.

Susan had watched the way Lisa and

Chet looked at each other. It reminded her of Steve and herself years earlier. She liked the confidence of Mitchell and the respectful way he treated Lisa. Will Tanning had called several times and had an abrasive manner. The conflict over the pressure from the Tannings to buy their land didn't help the situation either.

The meal, hot, tasty and filling, prepared Chet and Steve for a hard day's work. They discussed their plans over one more cup of coffee. With their stomachs full and rested from a good night's sleep, they walked over to the new trail as the sun peeked over the distant mountains. They were also ready for trouble. Both men carried handguns and kept loaded rifles nearby. They decided to clear the remainder of the rubble from under the former overhang and use it to level the area around the large boulder sitting in the ravine.

'Steve, we want anybody who might try and get up to the valley to think I'm alone so I best work on the exposed part of the trail.'

'I can level ground inside the hole. They won't spot me there.'

'That's good. You'll also be closer to Lisa or Susan on the other plateau if they need help.'

On the plateau above the passage Lisa sat in the shade of a large tree watching for approaching riders. Her mother sat beside her. In a couple of hours she planned to go back to the cabin to prepare lunch. The spot under the tree gave an expansive view of the ranchland to the west, north and south. Most of the land belonged to Tanning. His ranch-house lay out of sight on the other side of a distant rise.

An hour later Will Tanning and his four hired guns rode casually towards the Three Points. They crested the rise that hid the Tanning ranch from view. Will rode alongside McCall at the front of the group.

'You four look confident, like this sort of thing isn't new to you,' said Will.

'It's numbers, that's all. We know better than to take on a dozen armed men of average ability. But give us five on one against a gunslinger like Mitchell, especially when he's alone in an isolated canyon and we have the chance to surprise him, to us it's easy money.' McCall spit on the ground. 'Yep, easy money.'

'Do you expect Mitchell will watch for us?'

'Maybe, but we'll stop at the bottom of the ridge up ahead and we'll slip up to the thin passage before dark. It may be slow moving but we can't lose our way in the passage. Then we'll let him have it.'

Truman, Presson, and Lead Walker trailed behind and talked amongst themselves as they drew closer to the Points.

'One man trapped in a valley and he pays us each half a year's wages,' chuckled Truman. 'Them Tannings have too much money.'

'Might buy myself a spread with my

share,' Walker added. 'Maybe up north a bit.'

Presson wore a frown. 'Best keep your eyes open and concentrate on the job. This Mitchell's no fool.'

'He's one man, Billy. We'll be having us some fun at Cullimore's Saloon by tomorrow night,' Walker replied.

'I hope you're right, Lead. I hope you're right.' Presson moved his horse forward and rode alone for a time.

At the bottom of the ridge Will and McCall turned north while the others waited. Will and McCall followed the low ground until they had a view of the new entrance into the valley. They staked their horses at the bottom and moved out until they had a good view but still had the cover of the tops of the nearby trees. They saw one man moving rocks in the passage.

'There he is,' pointed McCall.

'Perfect, let's slip around and work our way to the entrance while we still have light.'

They retrieved their horses and

returned to the other men with Will Tanning leading as they rode up the hill. He liked the nerve of the men but couldn't get his mind off the self-confident actions of Mitchell and how he had humiliated him in front of Lisa Cullen. He knew the Three Points and the passage. He and his brothers had hiked up there in their younger days. He also knew it was easy to defend but didn't share this news with the others. He had already decided, on the advice of his father, that one of the gunmen would lead the way through the passage. He didn't care if one, two, or all of the gunmen died as long as Mitchell got his.

The ride and hike to the entrance of the passage brought heat and more heat. They staked their horses under the cover of the trees once the path grew too steep and continued on foot. All were feeling the heat and the water in their canteens eased the fatigue.

Lisa's whistle echoed through the valley. Susan picked up her gun and ran out the door. Steve arrived at the path leading to the plateau at the same time as her. Chet ran behind the cabin and picked up a sack sitting beside the house before joining Susan and Steve.

Chet spotted the gun in Susan's hand. 'Looks like you're ready to lend a hand, Susan.'

'I am at that.'

'She's a good shot. Has had plenty of practice,' added Steve.

'Good,' said Chet. 'We should give the Tannings all they can handle.'

Chet, Steve and Susan hurried up the path to join Lisa on the small plateau. They edged their way along the trees in order to stay out of view of the approaching riders, stopping beside Lisa in the shade of the large tree.

Chet squinted into the midday sun. 'Recognize them?'

'It's Will Tanning riding in front. I don't know the other riders,' Lisa replied.

Susan and Steve didn't recognize anyone except Tanning either.

'The others look ready for trouble, handguns and rifles,' Mitchell said, as he studied them through the field glasses.

Chet took the bag off his shoulder and set it on the ground. He opened it and pulled out a stick of dynamite and attached a fuse. 'I figure this should show them we mean business.'

Mitchell searched the plateau, stopping at an area of loose rocks a few feet away from the opening above the passage. He slid the stick of dynamite into a two-foot deep crevice in the ground on the opposite side of the loose rocks and running parallel to the passage. The ten-inch fuse lay on the ground like a snake.

He gave Lisa a box of matches. 'Think of this as our way of saying hello. It'll make plenty of noise and shower them with rocks without hurting them too much.'

'Hopefully, it'll send them back from where they came,' added Steve.

'When should I light it, Chet?' asked Lisa nervously.

Chet showed Susan and Lisa a spot towards the outside entrance to the passage and about thirty feet from the dynamite. He handed Susan a second stick of dynamite with a shorter fuse. 'Susan, you keep an eye on the path at this point and signal Lisa with a wave when they start through the passage. Lisa, you then light the fuse and you both high-tail it for cover behind those trees at the other end of the plateau. After the blast, hide yourselves near the small meadow, deeper in the woods to the north. Your pa and I will deal with them if they get stubborn and continue into the valley. Watch closely, but don't expect them to come at us until dark.'

'What do we do with this?' Susan held up the second stick of dynamite.

'That's for your escape if something goes wrong. Light the fuse and toss it. You'll have time to slip away after the explosion and get down the path. You can hide in the valley. Be sure to hunker down and stay quiet.'

Chet and Steve knew they had plenty

of time, so they set up two logs as cover in a spot that had a perfect view of the interior exit of the passage.

'Full moon tonight,' Chet said. 'We shouldn't have any problem seeing them.'

Cullen checked his rifle for the third time. 'We're ready.'

* * *

Will had climbed the trail and used the passage several times in his youth. He glanced at the sun. 'The climb will take about two hours. We'll stop just shy of the narrow opening and wait for darkness to make our move. We know Mitchell was at the new opening so we'll have the benefit of surprise. At the passage McCall and Presson will lead us through with Walker and Truman watching our backs.'

'Sounds like a comfortable place for you,' laughed Truman.

'We hired you for your guns. I'm a rancher, not a gunman.'

'Sure, Mr Rancher. Fact is, you have a reputation for knowing how to handle a gun.' Truman spit tobacco between Will's boots. 'It don't matter though. Just make sure the rest of our money is ready for us after the job is done.'

'It'll be there. A Tanning always pays his debts. Now let's climb.'

McCall and Presson moved along the last bit of trail through the trees on their way to the dark opening to the passage. The others followed through the winding trail. McCall, moving slowly and carefully in the lead, kept an eye on the trail with the help of the large moon. He noticed four sets of footprints in the soft soil: two sets of men's prints and two smaller sets, perhaps women or kids.

McCall put up his hand and stopped the rest of the group. He pointed at the footprints. 'Tanning, you want to explain why there are four sets of fresh prints on this trail?'

'Just locals, I expect. I came up here when I was young. Don't see why other youngsters wouldn't do the same.'

'Maybe, but let's keep an extra close eye. This is starting to smell bad.'

As the procession of men climbed the remainder of the path Will mulled over the possible owners of the other prints. Mitchell, new to the district, knew few people. In the immediate area only one group came to mind, the Cullens. Mitchell had met Lisa at least once and the two small footprints made sense. Will pictured Steve, Susan and Lisa Cullen climbing the trail to the high valley. His heart sank like the setting sun.

Will pursed his lips, his anger again taking control of him. He roughly pushed past Presson and McCall. 'When we move, I'll take the lead through the passage.'

'Suit yourself,' said McCall.

★   ★   ★

Chet and Steve waited patiently and quietly for the approaching trouble.

133

They knew that silence was their friend and dramatically improved their odds against five tough men. Chet liked the way Cullen held his rifle, like an extension of himself. It showed comfort and confidence.

The air cooled as the shadow of night pushed across the valley. Even under the blanket of moonlight Mitchell could imagine cattle grazing peacefully on the rich green grass.

On the plateau Lisa sat near the dynamite, watching the expansive vista of rangeland disappear under the shroud of night. Susan nervously waited and watched the area near the entrance to the passage, the full moon illuminating a jagged line on the floor mirroring the top of the passage. The strong light assured her that she could not miss the men passing by. She also took care to keep her head back far enough that it didn't form a shadow on the floor.

★　★　★

Will Tanning got to his feet and checked his gun. 'It's time.'

Tanning and the hired guns stepped softly as they neared the entrance to the passage.

7

The five men crept silently into the passage. Even in the slice of moonlight in the passage Susan recognized the outline of the first man as that of Will Tanning. She leaned well back from the crevice and looked at Lisa sitting beside the stick of dynamite. Susan gave the hand signal, just visible from Lisa's position. The match at the ready, Lisa waved back acknowledgment of the signal. Susan walked swiftly but quietly towards the trees at the other end of the plateau.

Lisa scraped the match across a flat rock. The match snapped in two. She grabbed the small box and removed another match. This one burst into flame as it scraped across the rock, the light masked from the direction of the passage by her cupped hand. She touched the end of the fuse with the flame. The fuse burned true and Lisa ran into the trees. She slouched down in the dark shadows but stiffened as a hand reached out and touched her shoulder.

'It's me, Lisa.' Susan's voice calmed her.

The fuse reached the stick of dynamite, the explosion shaking the plateau and sending rocks shooting towards the passage.

The walls inside the passage shook violently as rocks and stones rained down. Will Tanning dropped to the ground and McCall tripped over him in the darkness. Behind Tanning and McCall several larger pieces of rock fell along with the smaller pieces, forming a waist-high pile of rubble.

'We're going to get trapped in here!' shouted Truman.

Will regained his feet. 'Is everyone OK?'

'A few scratches is all,' said McCall.

'Same here.' Presson's voice came from near the pile of rubble.

'I'm fine,' said Truman, 'but I think Walker's dead.'

McCall squeezed past the other men and looked down at his old friend buried under the rubble, only his lifeless face and right arm visible. McCall looked up at the crack of light, his rifle pointed in the same direction.

'Tanning,' whispered McCall, 'we're sitting ducks in here. We either go back the way we came, or move forward to open ground in the valley. Whatever we do, we do it now.'

Will's mind filled with the embarrassment of another humiliating loss to Mitchell. 'We move forward.'

The four men moved as quickly as possible through the passage, watching above for falling rocks. Twenty minutes later a jagged strip of moonlight revealed the exit into the valley.

Chet and Steve rested on their elbows behind the logs, rifles pointed at the passage. The grass glistened with dew while a distant owl made the only noise. Both men knew that if Tanning and his gang had continued in the direction of the valley they would arrive shortly.

Will Tanning edged up to the end of the passage, careful to remain in the shadow. He craned his neck and saw some cover just inside the valley, a grove of thick trees on the left and a few large boulders on the right, both about twenty feet away. The difficulty would be getting there without finding hot lead in the gut.

McCall tapped Will on the shoulder. Will turned to find the gunman holding a two-foot wide piece of shale. McCall pointed to the ground and moved his fingers in a walking motion. He then pointed at himself and at the exit. Will nodded, and let the bigger man slip past him.

McCall dropped to the ground, the slab of rock held up in front of him. He edged forward, keeping himself behind the shale, and reached the end of the passage.

Chet and Steve kept their eyes locked

on the passage, the full moon providing a clear view. Chet glanced quickly at Steve, who looked back and nodded. Both men saw the moonlight reflecting off the piece of stone as it moved slowly forward. McCall's feet and lower legs showed from behind the rock for only brief instances, frustrating the abilities of Chet and Steve to get a clear shot. They did not want to miss with their first shots and give away their positions.

McCall resisted peeking around the sides of the stone. He looked left then right to gauge his position in relation to the boulders and trees. Several minutes passed as McCall eased his way completely out of the passage. He again surveyed the area. The trees provided excellent cover and easier access to other cover. However, rocks as big as a man's head dotted the ground between him and the trees, making access difficult. The boulders to his right provided solid but limited cover, and the level ground allowed easier approach, while maintaining a low profile. McCall dug his left foot into the ground. He pushed off and rolled towards the boulders while keeping the stone in front of him. Five feet away from the boulders he slammed to a stop, a stump of a small tree digging into his side. He winced in pain as he centered the flat rock in front of him and caught his breath.

Mitchell looked at Steve and pointed at himself, his eyes, and the opening to the passage. Then he pointed at Steve and the man behind the slab of shale. Mitchell knew Cullen was a crack shot and left him to deal with the man behind the rock while he kept watch on the passage.

Steve Cullen set his rifle barrel in a groove in the log below a branch, which provided cover for his head. He peered down the sight, watching the man behind the slab of stone adjust his position. The man started rolling towards the boulders again. Steve likened it to hitting a running deer, except he only had small parts of the target open and only for a split second.

He also knew he had to hit his target before it reached the cover of the tall boulders.

He recognized a pattern in the man's movements and followed the target before slowly squeezing the trigger. The flash from the rifle briefly illuminated Cullen's position. The rancher quickly ducked behind the log and moved a few feet to his right before looking up again.

McCall grunted in pain as he finished the last couple of rolls to the boulders. Behind the big boulders he inspected his leg. The bullet had entered just below his knee and exited near his ankle. He wrapped a bandanna around the exit wound and tied his belt tightly just above the entry wound.

Cullen had seen the man buckle after the shot and whispered, 'I got a piece of his leg, Chet.'

'That'll slow him down. Good work.'

McCall looked at his bleeding leg with concern but knew he had to give some cover to the others in order to get help. The leg throbbed as he moved over a few feet to take up position between two of the large boulders. He drew his two guns and aimed towards the most likely position for someone with a gun, the two fallen logs.

'Now!' yelled McCall to the men in the passage as he fired non-stop.

One of the bullets splintered the wood near Cullen. Will, Truman and Presson exploded out of the passage, Will and Truman toward the trees on the left, Presson towards the rocks and his friend McCall.

Chet's first shot missed Will's head by inches. His second shot caught Presson squarely in the chest. The gunman collapsed dead halfway to the boulders.

Will found cover behind the largest tree, bullets ricocheting off the bark and singing as they flew past his head. Truman tumbled the last few steps and joined Will among the trees but found the other trunks too thin to provide proper cover. He looked to his left where Will leaned his back against the big tree. The gunfire continued, missing Truman by inches. Cullen slowed his shooting and watched the man struggle to find cover.

'Tanning,' whispered Truman. 'You best move over. I'm taking that cover.' Truman propelled himself across the opening, preparing to push Tanning aside. Cullen fired as Truman leaped, the bullet passing through his neck. Truman fell dead at Will's feet.

Will squinted in the moonlight and saw Presson lying motionless on the ground thirty feet away and McCall grabbing at his wounded leg behind the boulders. He shook uncontrollably, knowing that he was basically alone. He breathed as best he could and calmed himself down.

'All right, Mitchell, we've had enough!' yelled Tanning.

'Throw out your guns, both of you, and no tricks,' replied Mitchell, keeping his head down in case Tanning was trying to find his position.

Tanning threw out his two guns.

McCall grudgingly did the same, knowing he needed medical treatment soon.

'All right. Now let's see those hands,' said Mitchell calmly. 'And remember, the slightest wrong move and we start shooting.'

Mitchell slid closer to Cullen. 'Steve, once they're in the open you keep your rifle on them. I'm going face-to-face with that coyote Tanning.'

Will Tanning, his hands held high in the air, walked out from behind the tree. 'McCall over there is hurt bad. I don't think he can stand.'

'Crawl out, stranger, and make it real slow-like. Remember, I can put a bullet in you real easy,' said Steve.

Will wasn't surprised to hear Cullen's voice. He seethed with anger but knew he couldn't do anything about it at this time. McCall crawled out from behind the boulder and stopped next to Tanning.

'Hands up, stranger,' said Cullen.

McCall raised his hands. Chet rose slowly and walked towards the two men. He glanced down at the two dead men.

'Where's the other one?'

'Dead in the passage,' replied Will. 'Rocks fell on him when you set off that explosion.'

'Let's just make sure.' Chet glanced over at Steve. 'Cover them.'

'Maybe you have him sitting in the shadows ready to dry gulch us. Let's fix that.' Chet aimed his Winchester at the passage and fired off six rounds.

Chet walked over and stood beside Steve. 'We've a heck of a mess here, Steve. Any ideas?'

Cullen looked at the two dead men. 'Well, these two can be the first two buried up here.'

Chet nodded. 'Tanning, there's a shovel over by that woodpile. You start digging. Steve, can you fix up that other fellow so he can make it out of here?'

'Can do.' Steve tied some bandages over the wounds and gave McCall a long stick with a 'Y' at the top to use as a crutch.

Will dug the holes and Steve helped him lower the two men in.

'These two have any family that should be told?' Chet asked McCall.

'Nah, they was both drifters with no home to speak of.'

'Now you two get a drink from the stream,' said Chet. 'Steve, why don't we get these two out of the valley?'

Lisa and Susan had watched the confrontation from above and joined Chet and Steve.

'Sounds good.' Steve smiled as he handed Susan his rifle and pulled out a hand gun.

Will glared at Lisa as she stood between her mother and father. He turned to face Mitchell. 'Mitchell, you'll get yours for the trouble you caused. That's a promise.'

'Just get moving.' Chet pointed his pistol at the passage. 'While you're at it, help your friend through.'

Will Tanning grabbed McCall's arm and guided him into the passage. Chet and Steve followed closely behind.

When they reached the rock pile where Walker lay, Chet walked up first and removed the dead man's gun and slipped it into his belt.

'Tanning, clear that pile of rocks.' Chet grinned.

'Soon, Mitchell, you'll get it real soon,' Will snarled as he uncovered Walker and cleared a narrow path.

Will helped McCall through the remainder of the passage. Steve carried Walker out and they moved slowly down the path to the horses. Steve draped and tied Walker over his saddle. Will lifted McCall into a saddle and mounted his own horse.

'Now get! And remember, this is private land. We won't be as nice if you try coming up here again,' said Chet.

Will Tanning looked back over his shoulder. 'Soon.'

Will and McCall moved slowly down the trail with a line of horses following. The last horse carried Walker's body. They soon moved out of sight in the darkness. Neither Mitchell nor Cullen, standing at the entrance to the passage, thought they had seen the last of the Tannings.

'I suspect they'll only be away a few days. The Tannings aren't ones for putting things off for long when they have their minds set on it,' Steve said.

'Steve, I think you're right. I also suspect we could use a few more men who want to teach the Tannings a lesson. Any ideas?'

'I believe so.' Steve scratched the stubble on his chin. 'I reckon John Hart and Nick Falconer would lend a hand; both are under the same pressure from Tanning to sell out and move.'

'Is that Jake Hart's pa?'

'Yup. You know him?'

'That fine young man saved my life when Will dry gulched me and left me to die in the sun.'

'They're good folk.'

'Why don't you get some shut-eye and go see them in the morning. Tell them straight that it's the same deal you and I have; and Steve, tell them it could be rough and to bring guns.'

While the Cullens slept Chet kept watch on the plateau overlooking the passage in case Tanning tried to return.

But Will Tanning had no interest in returning to the valley alone or with one injured man. He rode slowly, McCall riding beside him and cursing at the pain. Will reached into his saddle-bag and pulled out a bottle of whiskey he had planned to use to celebrate the death of Mitchell and the capture of the valley. He handed the bottle to McCall who grabbed it quickly.

McCall took a long pull and wiped his mouth with his sleeve. 'Ah, that helps. Now listen, Tanning, I expect to get all the money when we get back. You understand?'

'You'll get the money.' Will's thoughts quickly returned to the double embarrassment of losing the battle for the valley and losing Lisa Cullen. He had seen her at the exit to the passage standing close to Mitchell. Tanning shook with anger.

The two riders stopped at a slow-moving stream to water their horses. The sound of the water temporarily calmed Will. He felt sure he would win in the end. After all, his father would stop at nothing to own the valley. Then the two tired men continued their ride across the grassland.

The sun rose bright red as they neared the large ranch. Smoke from the cookhouse rode the wind, bringing the smell of frying bacon and eggs in their direction. The ranch hands walking to the cookhouse stopped dead in their tracks when they saw the two riders approach. Two men grabbed the reins of the horses ridden by Will and McCall. Two others helped McCall to the ground and carried him to the bunkhouse. Another two removed Walker from his last ride and took his body into the barn.

Dave Tanning awoke when he heard the horses arrive and the unusually loud voices in the area of the corrals. He did his best thinking over morning coffee and a private breakfast in the kitchen of his large ranch-house. He dressed and had his usual breakfast while waiting for Will to report. He ate very little and went to his office where he dropped into a leather chair and waited, coffee cup in hand.

Will walked up the steps of the ranch house and spotted his father through the office window. Even a glance at his son walking past the window told Dave that the news was disappointing.

Will walked into the kitchen and grabbed a cup of coffee out of the hand of the cook.

'Good morning, sir,' said the cook.

Will grunted and walked down the hall and into his father's office, where he fell into a leather chair across from his father.

Dave Tanning got up from his chair and walked to the window, his back to his son. 'Bad?'

'Yep. He hit us with dynamite and had help, the Cullens. We lost one man in the blast and two more in the shoot-out in the valley.'

'And Mitchell?'

'He seems set on trying to hold the valley. I expect he cleared a trail and managed to get across the water but I don't know how. It was dark and everything happened at the narrow passage and just inside the valley. My guess is he'll have cattle up there soon, real soon.'

'He wouldn't blow that hole without being prepared to move quickly to settle the valley. That's where he's been all this time.'

Dave Tanning turned and faced his son. 'Go get some sleep. There's lots to do. We'll talk with your brothers and come up with a plan. We're going to do whatever we have to in order to get our hands on that valley.'

*   *   *

The sun was new in the east as Steve Cullen left the passage. He mounted up

153

and kept a quick pace to limit his time away from the valley.

The small but neat Falconer ranch appeared in the distance. Cullen kept watching the horizon for approaching riders as he rode alongside the small creek that cut through Falconer's land, his source of water. His objective remained clear as he pulled up on the reins: get enough numbers together to confront Tanning. He noticed two new corrals outside the Falconer barn. Several young foals pranced around the corral nearest the barn. A powerful bull standing in the smaller corral kept a close eye on Cullen as he dismounted and tied his horse to the railing of the corral holding the horses. Nick Falconer also kept an eye on Cullen from the door of the loft of the barn.

Falconer's wife had died several months earlier and it had devastated Nick. Childless, he had only the small ranch left in his life and he swore he'd keep it in memory of his wife.

Falconer had tried several times to

work out a water-sharing plan with Tanning. Tanning would only talk about buying out his neighbor and wouldn't even discuss easing up on water use from the source of the vital creek. Falconer balked at each offer, despite his limit of eight hundred head of cattle. With more water he could raise three times that many and make a good living.

'Morning, Steve. Coffee's on if you're wanting.'

'Sounds fine, Nick.' Cullen patted his horse and followed Falconer into the small house. The sparsely furnished one-room cabin had the welcoming smell of fresh coffee. The neighbors sat at the small wooden table beside the cabin's only window. Falconer poured coffee and set the pot on the stove to his left.

'Good to see you, Steve. What brings you by?'

Cullen sipped his coffee and looked out at the Three Points in the distance. He relayed the water and land sharing plan, open to any of the small ranchers near the Points. He told Falconer about the confrontation the previous day and asked him if he wanted to join him and Mitchell.

'Well, I'll be — That explains the noise. I figured something big was happening but never would have guessed that.' Falconer got out of his chair and paced the floor. 'Sure. I like the plan. We could get one of the Hart boys to watch both our ranches. They can look after themselves with a gun.'

'Good idea. The younger Hart boy has been keeping a bit of a watch on my place already. Don't imagine stopping here as well would be a problem.'

'I've done my morning chores. We can stop by the Hart place on our way to the valley. I have to confess I'm curious to see that trail up there.'

Falconer strapped on his gun belt and grabbed his rifle. He went into the barn and moved a loose board aside. From the opening he pulled out an old shotgun and a box of shells. Cullen had heard that Falconer knew how to use a gun and he saw that in the confident way he handled the weapons. Falconer saddled up his best horse and rode across the grassland with Cullen.

The Hart ranch, a bit bigger than Falconer's, sat on the top of a small hill. The same river that ran through the Cullen land on its way to Tanning's spread sat at the bottom of the hill and behind the house. Dave Tanning worried that Hart would use too much and leave him lacking. Hart's problem was that half of his land was rocky and too steep for cattle to graze.

Hart and his wife Margaret had a large family, four boys and two girls, the youngest fifteen. Cullen and Falconer crossed the river and climbed the hill up to the house. The modest house seemed far too small to hold eight grown people. As Cullen and Falconer crested the hill they came upon John Hart and two of his sons tossing hay into a corral holding cows. In the distance two of the girls walked towards the house carrying baskets of fresh berries.

The visitors rode up to John Hart as he threw the last bale into the corral.

Hart shook hands with his visitors. 'Why don't you two water your horses and then join us in the house. Dinner's about ready.'

'Don't mind if we do,' Falconer smiled.

The horses drank deeply as Steve and Nick rubbed them down. When they had finished they walked into the house. The whole family sat at a large table in the middle of the room. They waved over the visitors and squeezed together to make room for them at the end of the table where John Hart sat.

'Howdy all,' smiled Steve. 'Margaret, that stew smells mighy fine.'

John Hart's wife blushed as she filled bowls with the piping hot food. 'Why thank you, Steve.'

'Saw you ride down from the Points this morning, Steve.' John Hart looked up from his food.

'That's what we came to talk to you about.' Steve and Nick relayed the plan and the agreement to share water and land. The Harts agreed to help out.

'I know young Jake has been keeping an eye on my place. We wonder if he can do the same for Nick while we get things settled with the Tannings?' asked Cullen.

John Hart looked over at sixteen-year-old Jake at the other end of the table. 'Well, son, you think you can handle it?'

'Sure, Pa.' Jake had youth as well as boundless energy.

Margaret cringed and walked over to her husband. 'John, there's no telling what those Tannings will do. Can we send Tommy along with Jake?'

'Good idea. You two make sure you're prepared for anything and keep your eyes open.'

'Yes, Pa, we can handle it,' said Jake.

All four boys had been brought up able to shoot. It was tough territory and John and Margaret wanted them ready for anything.

Jake and Tommy grabbed their guns and strapped them on. The other two sons who would keep an eye on the Hart land did the same.

Steve, John, and Nick mounted up and started on their way to the Points. They kept to the top of the ridge above the river that skirted the Hart land. From here they had a view of most of the grazing land. The afternoon sun was not their friend this day. It pounded down on them relentlessly. John Hart took off his hat and wiped his brow.

Hart's gaze locked on another hill in the distance where five riders moved in single file towards the Points. 'Looks like the Tannings still have their stubborn streak.'

'We best pick up the pace,' Cullen said. 'We have to make sure we get there before they do.'

8

The riders were indeed the Tannings, led by Dave Tanning himself, sitting high on his black. Behind him rode Alan and Luke. The long-serving, loyal cowhands Wellwood and Sanchez brought up the rear. Both cowhands knew their way around a ranch but could also handle a gun if need be.

Dave Tanning's powerful body sat comfortably on his big horse, his strength maintained by working on the ranch alongside his men five days a week. He believed he had worked hard to get his extensive holdings and wasn't about to give them up without a fight.

He had selected riders who knew the area well for he planned to learn how Mitchell intended to get cattle into the valley and then offer him twice what it was worth. Tanning knew that control of the source of the water for the area was as important as owning the rich grazing land. He couldn't imagine giving up that control to anyone, let alone a stranger. He hoped the cash offer would settle things, but kept his mind working on other options, deadly options. Tanning liked to be prepared.

Cullen, Falconer, and Hart moved quickly and arrived at the Three Points far ahead of the Tannings and their men. Cullen led the way up the gradually rising trail toward the narrow passage. He glanced over his shoulder where he was surprised to see the five Tanning riders turn north and cross the river.

'It seems they want to have a look around,' Steve said.

'I don't expect the trail up to the new entrance will be a secret much longer,' replied Falconer.

Susan had been on watch and had told Chet and Lisa what she had seen. Susan and Lisa returned to the plateau while Chet went to the new entrance and watched the riders approach while he kept out of sight in the shadows. He easily recognized the lead man as Dave Tanning. Just like Cullen, Mitchell wasn't surprised to see Dave Tanning have a look around. He didn't know what would follow though, as they rode up in daylight and in fairly small numbers. Mitchell thought it unlikely they would resort to gunplay without the advantage of surprise. He had seen a pattern in the Tannings, a pattern that led to mistrust on his part.

On the other side of the Points Cullen and his two neighbors arrived at the small meadow where they watered and fed their horses. They staked them near the other horses and mule and walked up to and through the passage. Susan met them at the other end and told them Chet was at the new passage.

Hart and Falconer's jaws dropped when they saw the giant 'U' forming the new entrance.

'Well, if that don't beat all,' said Hart.

'If I hadn't seen it I wouldn't believe it,' added Falconer.

Introductions were brief as the four men watched Dave Tanning and the others approach the forest near the entrance to the new trail.

The Tannings and the other men stopped their horses near the hidden entrance to the start of the new trail and looked around. Tanning got off his horse and walked back and forth in front of the trees. He bent down and inspected the grass in a small clearing just inside the trees.

'This grass has been cropped by horses, not cattle. Here are some horseshoe prints. Yep, someone has been keeping a horse or horses here. Let's have a look around deeper in the trees.'

In the valley Chet and the ranchers separated, Hart and Falconer on the plateau over the old passage, Mitchell and Cullen at the new opening.

'Want to get some rest, Chet, I can watch things here for a time?'

'Thanks, Steve, but I want to be here when things start up. I expect they've discovered the trail and my guess is that Tanning won't be happy. We'll see them when they arrive at that open area on the other side of the river gorge. When they get there let's fire off a few warning shots so they know they aren't welcome.' Chet patted his rifle.

Dave Tanning sent Alan and Luke ahead a short distance to scout around and they weren't gone more than five minutes before returning with news of the trail.

'Pa, we only got a short ways up,' panted Luke, 'but it looks gradual and wide, plenty of room for cattle if it's the same the rest of the way.'

'All right. Wellwood, Sanchez, get on up there and see what's ahead. We'll follow after a bit.'

The two ranch hands pushed through the trees and quickly found themselves on the trail. Just as the others had said, the trail proved an easy climb. As they zigzagged up the hillside they soon began to hear rushing water. Several minutes later the sound of the water pounded in their ears as they moved into the open area at the edge of the river gorge. They walked up and inspected the heavy railing on each side of the bridge.

Steve had his rifle comfortably resting on a branch of a tree on the left side of the outside of the new passage. He recognized the two men from the Tanning ranch. 'They're Tanning hands, Chet. One's named Sanchez, the taller fellow's Wellwood.'

'Gunhands?'

'No. They're cowpunchers, but tough men.'

'OK, you put a scare into them, near Wellwood. I'll keep my rifle trained on Sanchez in case they return fire.'

As Wellwood and Sanchez moved forward on the bridge the mist rose, conflicting with the powerful sunlight. Ten feet out onto the bridge a shot rang out and wood splintered on the railing near Wellwood's right hand.

Wellwood ducked and bolted towards the trees. 'Sanchez, take cover!'

Sanchez turned and dove into the trees near Wellwood. They skirted the edge of the path out of sight of Mitchell and Cullen and ran down the trail. They met the Tanning men near the bottom.

Dave Tanning calmly walked up to the panting men. 'Heard a shot. What happened?'

'The trail goes all the way up!' gasped Sanchez. 'We made it to a bridge across the river gorge. Then they fired on us.'

'How many men?' asked Alan Tanning.

'Don't know, but we saw three riders go up the trail. Not sure if one of them was Mitchell. If it wasn't, that makes four.'

Dave Tanning grimaced and shook his head. 'All right, back to the horses.' They rode back across the grassland, Chet and Steve watching from the opening.

'You think they got the message?' asked John Hart later as they ate in the cabin.

'Don't think so,' replied Chet.

At the Tanning ranch-house they also ate supper. The three sons ate in silence, giving their father plenty of time to think. The elder Tanning speared a potato and chewed it slowly. He looked around the table at his three sons. His eyes fell on Luke, who stayed calm in crisis situations but preferred working with cattle even though he was fast with the iron. He backed up his family but lacked the killer instinct. Alan, the middle son, was stubborn, serious, and fiercely dedicated to growing the Tanning fortune. He had the strength and reflexes to give any man a battle, but didn't know where or when to pick a fight. The youngest, Will, had the best potential to survive in this tough situation. He feared nobody. He also still battled his emotions and his youth, things that kept getting him into trouble. Yes, Dave Tanning saw himself when he was young reflected in Will.

Dave Tanning ate another a piece of

potato and set his fork on his plate. 'Boys, tomorrow I want you three to keep an eye on the ranch. I've got business to attend to.'

'Going to town, Pa?' asked Luke.

'No, I'm going to the hidden valley to talk business with Mitchell.'

'You can't do that, Pa!' shouted Will as he jumped to his feet. 'That Mitchell's a gunman. He'll kill you on the spot.'

'Sit yourself down, son. Mitchell is fast with the iron but he's not a cold-blooded killer.'

Will slumped back onto his chair. He knew his father was right. Both times he had had a run in with him, Mitchell was calm and calculating, not ready to shoot first. He also knew that Mitchell had possibly been faster than he was.

Early the next morning Dave Tanning sent Sanchez out to the barn to get the black ready. Then Tanning walked straight to his office where he unlocked the desk drawer and pulled out three thousand dollars. He stuffed the pile of cash into his saddle-bag and securely latched the clasp. He left the office as abruptly as he had arrived, his mind focused on settling things and getting things back to normal.

He walked down the steps from the veranda to where Sanchez held his horse. The saddle squeaked under his weight. He wore no holster and carried no rifle. Thoughts of a future without Mitchell and gaining control of the valley filled his mind. He took a wandering route, intentionally going past the other three ranches in the area. At the Cullen and Falconer ranch he saw one man at each, but neither owner. At the Hart ranch he saw nobody outside but some movement in the house. Several sets of hoof prints led from this, the closest ranch-house to the valley, in the direction of the Points.

Are they all working against me? Tanning asked himself. He wasn't sure but even so, combined they had far less land than he. But the longer he rode the more he believed that they were teaming up. He smiled to himself. *Fine, I'll double the offer to all of them, that'll tear them apart and get me their land. I can afford it with the extra money I'll make raising cattle in the valley.*

On the plateau over the passage John Hart stood watch. He scanned the horizon frequently for the first two hours and saw only cattle and deer. Once more he raised his field glasses and swept from left to right. Something coming straight at the Points caught his attention. He solidified his stance and looked again. A smile crossed his face. Dave Tanning, alone and unarmed, rode straight at him at a steady pace. Hart signaled the others, and all but Falconer, who remained on watch at the new entrance in case of a back attack, joined him on the plateau.

'Looks like we're in for some business talk.' Chet returned the field glasses to John. 'Don't see any other reason he would come up here alone and unarmed.'

'I'm settled in here good. He's wasting his time,' said Hart.

'But we may as well be neighborly. Let's meet him at the inside of the passage and hear what he has to say. We'll have Lisa and Susan on lookout just in case.'

Dave Tanning arrived at the outside of the passage two hours later. He staked his horse and squeezed his wide shoulders through the passage. He had visited the valley twenty years earlier and remembered green, lots of green. Despite the memory his jaw still dropped when he entered the valley. The lush expanse of grass seemed endless. He gathered himself before even bothering to acknowledge the four men standing in front of him.

'Coffee's on, Dave.' Mitchell pointed at the cabin and offered his hand. Tanning hesitated, then shook it and those of the other three.

Dave Tanning had become accustomed to people calling him Mr Tanning until he told them otherwise.

He let it pass. Owning the valley and controlling the water displaced all other thoughts. While the cabin was much too small for his liking, the setting beside the creek and with the mountains in the background made the plains setting of his ranch seem drab. As he climbed the stairs he stopped on the porch and looked to his right where the new entrance yawned before him. Plenty of room to move in cattle. His pulse rate increased.

Mitchell opened the heavy wooden door. 'Come on in and have a seat.'

'Obliged.' Tanning tried his hardest to sound civil sitting across from the men he hated. He saw that the cabin, while small, was well constructed, intended for long-term use. The small hand-made stone stove in the corner held a coffee pot. Tanning noticed a second door on one side that he had not noticed outside. It stood over three feet above the ground, too high to use except in an emergency, but ideally suited for adding to the size of the cabin. He understood that Mitchell had no plans to move and hoped his generous offer would convince him otherwise.

Mitchell grabbed the coffee pot and walked over to the table. He poured coffee for everyone. 'Hot and strong.'

Tanning shuffled uneasily in his chair, looking across at the other ranchers at the table. Tanning had grown used to dominating in all parts of his life and didn't like being outnumbered. He knew his strength rested in the saddle-bag sitting on the floor next to his chair.

'Well,' Chet looked Tanning straight in the eye. 'I don't reckon you rode all the way up here for the coffee. What can we do for you?'

Tanning stared right back. 'Right to the point; I like that.'

Tanning reached down and lifted his saddle-bag onto his lap. Instinctively, the other men moved their hands closer to their guns. Tanning reached into the bag and pulled out a stack of money and set it on the table. He didn't like the confident look on the faces of the four men and decided to increase the offer.

'I'm prepared to offer each of you triple the value of your land: cash. That's money worth thinking about.'

'I give you credit for coming up here alone and unarmed. Still, I've become mighty attached to this piece of land and plan to raise cattle on it for many years to come,' Mitchell said.

Tanning's face reddened. 'And you three? It'll take years for you to make back this kind of money! Come to your senses.'

Cullen, Hart, and Falconer all declined the offer instantly.

'Now, gentlemen, let's not be too hasty. This is an offer most would jump at.'

Tanning's comments were met with powerful silence. He took a deep breath and packed the money back in his saddle-bag. In his own silent statement Tanning eased himself out of the chair, through the door and down the steps from the porch. The four ranchers watched him slowly make his way to the passage. Chet thought it was a little too slow. He watched Tanning study the perimeter of the entire valley as he walked.

'It looks like he's scouting; probably has other ideas,' said Falconer.

'Afraid so,' Mitchell replied. 'We best be prepared.'

Tanning saw movement above the passage, a woman with a scattergun in hand. He saw no other lookouts but was certain there was someone watching the new entrance. On the walk through the passage Tanning decided that the valley was too difficult to attack. He mounted his horse and set out for home. On the ride he decided that getting Mitchell was the key, and he would use one of Mitchell's own ideas to get him. Something used when they tried to attack the valley in force. His spirits lifted, and as if it could sense it, his black quickened its pace.

The work on the trail and entrance moved quickly with extra hands to help keep watch as well as work. The leveling of the top of the trail took only two days. The railings over the ravine and the clearing of a few trees that had fallen also went quickly. Lisa worked side-by-side with Chet, topping the rocky surface with soft soil. Three days later, the finishing work complete, the trail and the valley were ready for the first herd of cattle.

Tired but content, Chet sipped water from a ladle in the cabin. 'That was good work. With the new trail complete I suspect it's time for one more task before we concentrate on raising cattle. With our agreement to share our lands until we all get larger spreads, we should make this valley easier to defend.'

'What did you have in mind, Chet?' asked John.

'I think we should close the old passage permanently. This valley would be much easier to defend with only one access point available.'

'Makes sense, Chet,' nodded Cullen.

'Anything I can do to help?' asked Hart.

'You bet, John. I need you to take the last walk through the passage and bring the horses and my mule around and into the valley.'

Everyone agreed with the plan. John Hart grabbed his rifle and entered the passage. Chet walked outside the cabin and into the cool woods behind. Here he bent down over the wooden box. He opened the box and removed six sticks of dynamite. With the explosives in his pocket he walked towards the path leading to the plateau. He climbed the hill and found Lisa in the shade of a tree watching the horizon.

'Hi, Lisa.'

Lisa smiled and got to her feet. 'Hi, Chet. Here to take over?'

'Nope. We're going to close this passage permanently. Easier to defend the land that way.'

'Makes sense.'

'John is moving the horses. Now, if you could watch for John on the rangeland I'll get the dynamite ready.'

'I'll let you know when he's out of the way.'

Chet walked near where Lisa and Susan had set off the dynamite the previous time and found several new cracks had developed after the blast. He selected an exceptionally wide crack well back from the passage that had smaller cracks extending to the passage at wide angles.

'There goes Mr Hart.' Lisa said as she walked over to Chet.

'Good. It's all clear.' He stuffed the six sticks into the crack. Once again he used a long fuse. Once lit, he and Lisa ducked behind trees at the farther end of the small meadow.

The fuse crackled and spit fire until it reached the dynamite. The explosion shook the whole plateau. Fifteen feet of the surface shifted towards the passage, sealing it tightly. Dust and small rocks flew into the air from the half-moon crater formed where the dynamite had sat.

Chet came out from behind the trees with Lisa nervously holding his arm. Chet smiled. 'It's all right. I've been working with this stuff since I was ten.'

They inspected the area and determined that the explosion had totally sealed the passage and a tall wall of rock prevented access to the plateau from the outside.

John Hart, out on the grassland with the line of animals, ducked instinctively when the explosion erupted. The horses reared a bit but he was able to control them and keep the long line moving. He crossed the river and entered the cleared access to the new trail.

'Come on now,' Hart said to the horses. 'Let's break in this new trail.'

Back on the plateau Chet and Lisa soaked in the calm after the noise of the explosion. They looked out over the green valley. This was the time that Chet decided that soon he would ask Lisa to be his wife. He had little experience with romance, but as with many other things in his life he trusted his instincts. In this case he fully trusted them. It just felt right. He wanted to ask her now but knew that he must do one more thing first. Settling matters with Tanning was the priority. He knew he would have to do what had to be done to keep this valley, his home: his and Lisa's home, he hoped.

The noise from the explosion caught the attention of everyone at the Tanning ranch. Cowboys gathered beside a corral full of cattle and looked east.

The front door to the ranch-house opened and the Tanning boys filed out and stood on the veranda, cursing Mitchell and the others. Dave Tanning, the only one not frustrated, joined them. He carried a rolled-up piece of paper under his arm.

Will turned to face his father. 'Pa, those four men could hold off a small army.'

'Yep,' replied Dave Tanning with a grin on his face. 'And I expect that blast has made it even tougher.'

'How so?' asked Luke.

'Based on where that dust is rising from and the size of the blast, I figure Mitchell and the others have just sealed off the old passage.'

'Damn!' shouted Alan, 'That leaves only one way to get at them, that new trail.'

'That's what I hope they think,' Dave Tanning grinned.

The older Tanning unrolled the paper on the small table on the veranda. The map had frayed edges and looked very old. The three sons gathered around and looked down at the hand-drawn map of the Three Points. They recognized notes in their father's handwriting.

'I drew this map with the help of an Indian scout who worked for me when your ma and me first settled here. It shows another way to get into the valley.'

Alan was fascinated and pointed. 'I see the passage here . . . and here's the wall with the new entrance . . . but what is this?' Alan stopped his finger at a line going up the third wall.

'That, my boys, is the answer. It's an ancient trail used before the narrow passage was discovered. It's a tough climb, tried by many, completed by only a handful.'

'Aw, that Indian was feeding you a story,' scoffed Luke.

'I thought the same at first. But it's there. I gave it a try myself when I was about your age. I made it a quarter of the way before the rains came and forced me back. Much of the climb is rock and if they get wet . . . well, you're finished. Never gave it another try but knew I could have made it had it stayed dry.'

Dave Tanning flipped over the map. 'Here's a more detailed close-up drawing done by the Indian himself.'

'Pa, I want to be the one to go. I have a score to settle with Mitchell.' said Will.

'And I'll go with him,' said Alan.

Dave Tanning leaned his giant left hand on the railing and looked at the clouds moving over the Three Points.

'Don't know if I want to risk my own blood on this. I was thinking of hiring a couple of professionals to handle it. But it might work to our advantage for you two to go, seeing that there are others besides Mitchell up there. Falconer, Cullen, and Hart have good reputations in the area and we'd look real bad if word got out that it was us. If we handle it quietly ourselves it would be better. Right! You two go and get rid of them, but make it look like a robbery . . . take horses and any other valuables and get rid of them somewhere.'

'Then it's settled.' Will ran into the house.

Dave Tanning walked over to Alan and put his hand on his shoulder. 'Alan, keep an eye on your younger brother, he still lets his emotions run him.'

'I will, Pa, don't worry.'

'Good. Now you and Will get to town and get whatever supplies you will need for the climb. Make sure you're ready to go at the end of the week. We don't want to give them too much free time.'

184

9

In the valley, John Hart, Steve Cullen and Chet Mitchell finished topping the rough rock base with another layer of soil and constructed the last of the fences and gates in the valley. Nick Falconer took time away from the valley the first day to check on the three ranches. When he found everything in order he slipped quickly into town to buy supplies. He avoided the Tanning boys but expected they would soon know that he was there, so he left quickly and returned to the valley.

The next two days saw the building of a barn next to the cabin. The only domestic animals in the valley, the horses and mule, contentedly cropped grass in the shade of one of the mountains. On the second day Hart rode down the new trail and promptly returned with a welcome side of beef and some vegetables.

Two people remained on guard on the lookout spot over the new entrance. They all knew that Tanning did not give up easily and this valley was something he wanted desperately. During the midday meal the men discussed cattle and Chet learned that he had partnered up with knowledgeable men. They had had to learn a few tricks, having limited land and a ruthless neighbor in Tanning.

Chet spent his free evenings with Lisa, walking around the valley or sitting on the porch. Two days later most everyone was on edge worrying about the potential attack by Tanning. Was he spending big money to hire more guns to take the valley?

After another day the tension increased further. Chet saw this, and he gathered everyone together except Hart, who remained on watch during the meeting.

'Folks,' Chet said, 'it's time we try and find out what Tanning is up to. I'm going to catch some shut-eye this

186

afternoon and go to the Tanning place and have a look around tonight.'

Lisa shuddered. 'Chet, that sounds dangerous.'

Chet placed his hand on hers. 'Now don't you worry, Lisa. When I was young, the local Indians taught me how to move in silence. I'll be in and out of there without them even knowing.'

That afternoon Mitchell leaned back against a tree on a slight rise just the other side of the creek from the cabin. He took in the view, imagining cattle dotting the green expanse. Soon he slept, as the warm breeze gently rustled the leaves overhead.

Later, Falconer kept watch over the entrance as Chet saddled his roan. The roan was restless to move after so many days at rest. Nick touched the brim of his hat as Chet rode past and Chet replied in the same manner.

A pale slice of moon stared down, giving Chet just enough light to make his way through the trail. The scant light made moving around unseen easier and this pleased both Chet and the others in the valley who were worried for him. He kept low and out of sight by following the winding river. Only cattle and deer crossed his path. Halfway across the Tanning land the whinny of a horse echoed through the shallow river valley. Chet ducked behind some trees and watched carefully, his hand instinctively dropping down to his Colt. A few minutes later a Tanning hand that had been watering his horse moved back up to higher ground and continued across the large spread.

Two miles further downstream the river turned sharply south. Mitchell dismounted and crawled to the top of the shallow valley where he patiently looked and listened. Ten minutes later, certain he was alone, he mounted the roan and continued towards the Tannings.

When he had closed to within a mile of the ranch he searched for and found a thick grove of trees in which to hide the horse. Now tied to a low bush, the roan ate grass. Chet contemplated the rifle hanging by his saddle. He reluctantly left it with the horse, concerned that moonlight reflecting off the steel barrel might give his position away. Sitting on a fallen log, Chet replaced his boots with moccasins he carried in his saddle-bag.

He stood up and checked his readiness. The dark clothes and soft shoes were both ideal for the night's task. He checked his handguns and found them loaded and in perfect working order.

The walk through the trees began as the Indians had taught him, on soft pine needles where possible and avoiding twigs and dry leaves. The going was slow but silent. He stayed in the cover of the trees as long as possible but soon came to the edge of the grove. The buildings of the Tanning ranch sat dark and unmoving in the distance. He kept in a crouch and moved very slowly as he crossed the rangeland. A few cows turned their heads in his direction as he passed, but then returned to resting.

Chet expected one or two cowhands on watch during the night, so he approached with great caution. He crawled the last few hundred feet, stopping beside a fencepost and several bales of hay in the corner of an empty corral. Nothing moved, but Chet knew that sitting in the shadows provided the best place to keep an eye on the yard. The eight buildings and grove of trees provided plenty of places for a man to sit quietly and watch for approaching trouble. Time moved slowly as he crouched on the dew-covered grass.

Twenty minutes later the distinct sound of wood rubbing on wood filled the peaceful night. In the wedge of darkness beside the cookhouse a cowhand pushed his chair back on a small wooden platform beside the porch. He moved into the light, a rifle in one hand and a tin cup in the other. The tall man took a swig of coffee and winced. He spit the coffee onto the ground and then dumped the remains of his cup in the same spot. He gave the area a lethargic glance and walked into the warmth of the cookhouse.

With sweeping checks of the rest of the yard and regular glances at the cookhouse door, Chet moved slowly along the fence, heading towards the large barn. The first thirty feet along the corral fence provided plenty of cover and fast progress. The remaining forty feet provided more of a challenge. Following the fence on the north side exposed him to view from the cookhouse. Chet elected to crawl across the fences on the outside. This route took longer but reduced the risk of giving away his position as the far end of the two corrals touched the corner of the barn. A large door for moving cattle and a smaller door were on the wall facing the cookhouse. Chet moved quickly through the shadow to the small door on the wall of the barn facing away from the yard and opposite a patch of trees.

A two-foot-long board fastened to the door with one bolt had a wooden handle near the edge of the door. The board extended past the door and rested in a bracket on the frame of the door. Chet lifted it slowly and pulled open the door. He entered, closed the door and stopped in the darkness against the wall inside the barn. He waited until his eyes grew accustomed to the darkness, in case cowhands might be sleeping in the barn. Once his eyes adjusted to the low light he methodically looked around and saw that he was alone.

He began a meticulous search of the barn for a hint of what the Tannings had planned. He found well-maintained stalls holding horses with a saddle, bridle, and blanket sitting on a wooden rail outside each stall. Firewood filled much of the far wall. The opposite end of the barn held another large door accessing the yard. The remainder of the wall holding this door contained a wooden workbench and shelving containing old saddles, broken spurs, and moth-eaten blankets. The workbench contained ranching essentials like leather oil, nails, and rope.

Chet didn't spot anything unusual until he saw boxes on the floor containing new items from the general store. The boxes held rolls of rope, but thinner rope than typically used by cowboys. The boots in the other box were not the type worn by riders. These boots had heavy sides for support and thick, heavily gripped soles.

An idea began forming in Chet's mind that would explain these strange purchases. He opened the bag at the bottom of the box containing the two pairs of boots and knew he had figured out what the Tannings had planned. The bag contained twenty-four heavy pins with loops on the end; loops just big enough to hold the thin rope in the other box. Chet had seen this type of equipment used in the mountains near the gold mines; men used them to pound into the rock to hold rope to assist in climbing the steep rock faces.

This convinced him that the Tannings planned a surprise attack over one of the tall cliffs guarding the valley.

As Mitchell returned the rope to the box he heard the shuffle of boots on gravel just outside the barn. He ducked into deep shadow near the shelving and drew his gun. Through the small window he saw a middle-aged man crossing from the bunkhouse toward the cookhouse. He wore no gun and carried a large frying pan in his left hand. The cook continued past the window and into the side door of the cookhouse to start preparations for the men who would climb out of bed at sunrise. The lookout came out of the front of the cookhouse a few minutes later with steaming coffee in his cup. He walked across the open area and leaned against a railing of one of the corrals. Here he sipped coffee and stared out into the darkness.

Chet cautiously crossed the barn and exited by the same door through which he had entered. Darting from shadow to shadow, he carefully worked his way back along the corral containing the fences beside which he had crawled earlier. Mitchell again crawled through the open land in the opposite direction from the watchman, but sticking to the shadowed low areas until he reached the nearby woods. He found himself on the opposite side of the ranch from his horse and slipped slowly along the low areas, keeping out of sight of the man with the rifle until he arrived at his roan. He rode slowly towards the Three Points and up the trail, arriving at the entrance as the sun winked above the mountains. John Hart waved as Chet entered the valley.

Over breakfast he told the others what he had found in the barn. 'I think the mountains are too high for what they're planning, so I'm going to have a good look around the third cliff. It's a heck of a climb, but possible with the gear I saw.'

'How will you climb it?' asked Lisa.

'I grew up in the mountains. I can't

climb sheer cliffs, but with a rope I can climb most anything else. Besides, I'm not expecting to climb it all, just see what's possible so we can take precautions.'

The next morning, being cautious, men stationed themselves in bushes in the two most likely spots someone might climb to gain access to the valley. Mitchell again saddled the roan and briskly rode out the new trail. This time he turned the other direction and headed towards the third cliff, a jagged, long face of rock between two of the mountains. The ends of the wall of rock had a substantially steeper access compared to the other two walls between the mountains and showed evidence of frequent rock slides from the steep mountainsides on each end.

Chet left his roan behind two enormous rocks on the edge of the steep terrain leading to the wall itself. The tall boulders gave plenty of shade and green grass grew in the shadows, providing food for the horse.

Looking up at the massive wall from the bottom of the access hill made Mitchell wonder if it was really possible to enter the valley from this side. He pushed on, carefully studying the area for any possible access points to begin the climb. There were several giant outcroppings of rock well below the wall itself, which prevented direct access at these places. Only between these outcroppings could someone even start to approach the main cliff face.

Chet took the first of these few access points and started the climb with a coil of rope over his shoulder. He edged his way through the brush, looking carefully for any signs of previous visitors, while limiting evidence of his having visited the area. He saw no signs, but covered over forty feet before the lie of the land forced him to the right. This brought him to the main cliff, a slab of wall as smooth as a lake on a calm day. Close examination revealed solid granite, lacking any cracks or indentations into which to drive a climbing pin.

He backtracked to the bottom and passed several more impassible outcroppings before coming to another possible access point. This one had a narrow passage used by small animals. This route took him through even steeper terrain to start. The bushes, trees and undergrowth thickened, and with painstaking slowness Mitchell worked his way through the forest. Several hours later he arrived at the wall. This time the wall contained a few imperfections allowing for foot and hand holds which, along with the pins, showed possibilities. However, when he moved in close to the wall he found the cliff face moved outwards the higher you went. Near the top the angle was so great that even the best climber he had ever seen in the mountains would have been unable to climb it.

Chet rested here under the shade of the cliff. He drank from his small canteen and looked down the slope. He had passed the halfway mark on the access area to the cliff.

Mitchell walked back down to the grassland, leaving as few footprints as possible. On the grassland he brushed a handful of branches over the ground to erase these footprints.

He passed another outcropping of tall rock formations limiting access to all but birds and very small animals. Between this point and the steep high side of the mountain remained one more possible access point. The area again contained heavy brush cover and many fallen trees, but Mitchell slowly made progress. At the midpoint in the climb to the foot of the cliff, he found an area of lower brush. He carefully moved the brush aside so as not to break any branches and studied the ground beneath.

A circle of rocks stared back at him like a giant eye. Amongst the green growth sprouting out of the middle lay old charred pieces of wood. Mitchell looked at what appeared to be another rock outside the circle. Something looked different about it so he brushed aside the dirt that had built up around it over the years and picked it up. He examined closely the Indian cooking pot with its wave-patterned rim and charred bottom from years of sitting on fires. Chet had seen remains of similar pots in the valley. He knew Indians had at least traveled this far up the slope.

He continued climbing, finding only two possible paths. The first turned back down the slope after running into a tall rock outcropping. He retraced his steps and started up the last possible trail. While starting out sharply, the trail led to another small flat area hidden in the trees before continuing on to the base of the steep, tall cliff.

The cliff again had a smooth texture but also included a narrow crack pushing upwards, starting three feet above where Mitchell stood. He could grab the crevice but had no footing to help him up. On the ground under the crevice laid a log, clearly cut by an axe. One end of the log had been cut at about a forty-five degree angle. Marks from the end of the log four feet up the wall showed how the Indians reached the first foothold. The rotten log could no longer support any weight so Chet made a pile of other rocks and smaller logs and climbed onto it to inspect the crevice.

He saw a narrow wedge just wide enough for a foot, but with smooth sides and no support on the gradually narrowing bottom. On closer inspection he found a piece of wood at the bottom of the crevice shaped in a triangle and about eighteen inches long. Like the log it had rotted but still held its form. Again marks in the crevice about two feet from the bottom showed where the wood had been wedged in and used as a foothold. Further up the crevice, where it widened to about a foot, small rocks jutted out, their tops chiseled away to form a flat surface. The crevice had smaller cracks and pitting, easily passable with climbing gear and pins. All one would need was time.

Chet moved the materials he had

stood on and swept away the footprints from the grass with his hand so that only the most experienced tracker could tell he had been there. Chet studied the area and memorized the placing of the small clearing and the crevice so that he could spot it from above.

The roan bobbed its head when Chet appeared, ready to move. Mitchell returned the way he had come, arriving at the entrance to the trail to find Steve Cullen finishing erecting two log fences which protruded at forty-five degree angles from each side of the trail entrance where it started on the rangeland.

Steve removed his hat and wiped his brow. 'Hi, Chet. I thought I'd finish this fence we talked about to help guide in the cattle.'

'That's fine work, Steve.' Chet saw Steve's rifle leaning against a nearby tree. 'Any trouble while I was away?'

'Naa, quiet as a church mouse. You find anything interesting?'

Cullen climbed on his horse and rode side-by-side up the trail with Mitchell as he learned the story of the ancient access route to the valley. The echo of the horses' hoofs across the wooden bridge caught Falconer's attention as he was putting the final touches to the entrance at the top.

Cullen replaced Falconer on watch at the entrance and Chet and Falconer returned to the cabin. Over dinner Chet relayed the story of the climbing trail up the cliff. The hot meal gave Chet new energy, and after dinner he invited Lisa to join him as he looked for the top of the wall above the access point.

They saddled two horses and headed out across the grassland. Chet calculated the spot was just about directly across from where he had built the cabin.

The green grass waved in the evening breeze as they crossed the closest bridge over a creek.

'I think that this valley is the prettiest thing I've ever seen,' said Lisa.

Chet looked over at Lisa and smiled. 'It's the second prettiest thing I've ever seen.'

Lisa blushed and smiled back.

The summer sun kept the evening bright as they neared the interior of the cliff. On the valley side of the cliff, the climb, while not very steep, required a good grip on bushes to help ascend. Chet found a narrow goat trail angling upwards and helped Lisa onto it. They walked single file along two levels of the path before the path ended with a steep fall-off. Chet crouched and looked under the ground cover of the steeper area. He pushed some brush aside and waved Lisa over.

'What do you see here?' Chet asked, as he pointed up the hill.

Lisa looked at the ground and her eyes saw a pattern of indentations. 'Why, these are steps carved into the hill!'

'Exactly.' Chet smiled. 'By the looks of it the rest of the climb will be easy.'

Chet used a flat rock to clean off the

dirt and plant growth that had collected on the steps over the years and soon they were at the top of the cliff. At the top they found a flat area extending most of the way from one end of the cliff to the other. In an area protected by a group of trees sat another circle of rocks from fires lit long ago. The young couple stood and admired the view of both the valley and the grazing land that included the Cullen ranch.

'It's a spectacular valley. I can't tell you how happy everyone is at your kind offer of sharing the grass up here in the dry summer months.'

'I'm happy to do it. After all, if I'm going to raise a decent number of cattle I'll need the use of the land off the valley in the cooler months, when grass grows slower at this altitude. It's fair and that's the way it should be.'

Lisa looked up at Chet as he scanned the valley. She could tell he meant every word he said. Her heart ached at the idea of leaving the valley.

Chet estimated the spot where the

crevice should be and leaned over the outside edge of the cliff. From this height it seemed inconceivable that anyone could manage the climb. He recognized the area below and saw the thin crevice. The foot and handholds reached most of the way up the rock wall. The crevice grew deeper the higher it got but the holds were towards the edge. The last one before reaching the top was about five feet down but within reach of overhanging brush, almost certainly used as the final handhold before arriving at the top. About three feet below the top of the cliff a hole had been chipped into the wall as a final foothold.

Mitchell sat on the edge of the cliff beside Lisa. 'I think we can set up a heck of a surprise for anyone trying to get into the valley this way.'

'How so?'

'Well, we'll need somebody up here to keep watch but I can rig up something that'll announce the arrival of a climber and make him regret climbing the wall.'

From bushes out of sight of a climber, Mitchell cut off several lengths of branches the diameter of a finger. He cut these into twelve-inch-long pieces and sharpened them on one end. Next, Chet cut a longer, thicker branch and trimmed off the smaller branches. He bent it several times and found it very flexible. With the tip of his knife he dug ten lined up holes slightly smaller than the sharpened sticks at one end of the longer branch. With a rock he pounded the sharpened sticks through the holes until they formed what looked like a giant comb.

He wedged the end of the thicker branch opposite the sharp sticks under a root sticking out of the ground, a foot away from the point above the climbing crevice. The tines of the giant comb stuck well out over the edge of the cliff directly over the crevice. Chet jammed thick sticks and rocks under the root around the end of the long stick, securing it tightly. He pulled the branch back until it stood straight up. The branch quivered under the strain until Chet let go. The branch shot forward, the sharp sticks hitting the area several feet below the last handhold in the crevice.

Chet cut one more stick, this one about eight inches long. He rounded both ends of the stick and leaned over the edge of the cliff. With a small pick he carved out holes on each side of the top of the last handhold in the shadows of the crevice. He held down the stick and found it about an inch too long. More carving brought it down until it just fit into the little holes but easily slid out. Mitchell tied the rope he had brought to the tip of the branch with the sharp sticks and fed it around a thin tree behind the root holding the other end of the stick.

'Lisa, pull that branch back until it nearly touches the ground.'

Lisa pulled back the branch while Chet marked where the rope reached the top of the last handhold. He cut the rope and tied it to the small stick. Lisa again pulled back on the branch and Chet slipped the stick into the two small holes over the handhold out of sight of a climber. He pulled it out several times, confirming that it would easily release if touched by a hand. The rope extended up and over the edge of the cliff, most of it in the darkness of the crevice. Chet draped some nearby vines over the portion of the rope that was exposed to view.

'All right, Lisa, ease up on the branch until the rope is tight: real easy now.'

'Right.' Lisa slowly lifted the end of the branch off the ground. When it reached twelve inches away the rope went taut, vibrating slightly but holding.

'That should do it, Lisa. When someone reaches up to grab that last handhold they'll release the branch and have a big surprise.'

The men alternated watch on the cliff, knowing that Tanning wouldn't wait long to get his hands on the valley, as the weather was growing warmer and the grass on the plains was beginning to dry.

During the day the men kept their guns handy while working on the cattle trail, while Lisa and Susan watched for approaching riders. Only twice did Tanning men ride near the trail but they never came close to entering. Dave Tanning had sent them to keep an eye on things from a distance and to distract the people in the valley from his real plan, a sneak attack up the steep rock wall using the climbing gear. He did not know that the ranchers knew about the surprise attack and that they all despised Tanning even more for planning such a cowardly assault.

Two nights later Chet climbed onto his roan and rode across the valley in preparation for his turn at watch. He climbed the path to the top of the cliff and found John Hart sitting against a tree, staring into the darkness.

'All quiet, John?'

'Yup. A bit surprised though. Up

until now the Tannings have moved quickly.'

'I think it won't be long. My guess is they've taken a few days hoping we would let our guard down.'

'Hope you're right.' Hart picked up his rifle and started down the hill.

Mitchell spread out his bedroll and inspected the rope and branch. Everything looked fine so he lay down on the bedroll and stared at the blanket of stars above. After a time his eyes shut and he fell into a light sleep. Two hours had passed in what seemed an instant when the sound of rustling bushes at the base of the rock wall awakened him.

10

Chet grabbed his rifle that was lying by his side and then remained motionless and silent. Another twig snapped, the sound again coming from outside the valley and at the base of the cliff.

With utmost care Chet crawled toward the edge, his hat left behind on the bedroll so that he would not be easily spotted looking down. In a place free of rocks or soil he peeked over the edge. At the base two men walked about in the starlight. Chet did not know who they were, but was certain he knew who sent them. Chet smiled at the clumsiness of the men. They must not expect that he and the others had any idea they would try this route into the valley.

They looked down at a piece of paper and back up at the cliff. One man pointed up. The men put the map away and collected wood, piling it up against the cliff. One man jammed one of the climbing pins into a crack two feet above the woodpile and another six feet higher. With the coil of thin rope slung over his shoulder, he gripped the higher pin and the edge of the crevice and started the long climb. He moved smoothly, twice stopping to wedge in two more pins for hand and foot holds. Chet moved to his left, the branches covering the rope also hiding him from the approaching man. The climber proceeded slowly but steadily, making a noise as he tapped more pins into the granite wall.

Halfway up, the man stopped and pulled the rope off his shoulder. With one hand gripping a pin, his other hand gracefully swung the rope and sent it sailing towards the top of the cliff. It hit its mark, a tree hanging over the edge at Mitchell's right. The thin, strong line draped over the tree and dangled beside the climber. He let the remainder of the coil in his hand fall to the ground and tied the other end around his waist. The man at the bottom held the rope tight, supporting the other man as he continued his climb.

With the extra support he moved more quickly now, nearing the stick resting in the shadow on top of the handhold, a few feet below the top of the cliff. Chet backed away and gripped his rifle. With the support of the rope the man might not use all the handholds, and he needed to be prepared. The climber might draw his gun as he topped the cliff.

As the man searched for footholds, the sound of his feet drew closer. Chet knew he must be near the handhold hiding the stick. He looked at the rope and remained motionless. Moments later the sound of the stick slipping out of its hold filled the air. The rope became a blur as the branch shot forward, disappearing over the edge of the cliff.

The thud of the sharpened sticks hitting something was quickly followed by a loud scream.

'Alan, they had a trap. I'm bleeding bad!' yelled Will, sounding as if he was standing beside Mitchell.

'I'll lower you down,' called Alan.

'Hold on, I have three small spears in my shoulder. I have to get them out first.'

Chet watched the branch shake and then swing free, bouncing up and down above Will Tanning's head.

'All right, bring me down; but slowly.'

The rope slid against the branch to the right of Mitchell. A smile crossed his face as he picked up a small axe and chopped through the branch, sending it and Will crashing to the ground. Chet heard a moan come from Will Tanning.

'Some skunk cut through the branch, Will,' exclaimed Alan. 'Can you stand?'

'I can stand. He didn't get my shooting hand. Let's let him have it.'

Shots tore through the air, some hitting the edge of the cliff. 'I don't see anybody, Will,' Alan said.

Will had his gun aimed at the top of the cliff but could see nothing. 'Just help me down the hill. We'll get that Mitchell, I swear it.'

Mitchell shifted further to his left and chanced a glance down the cliff. He saw the faint outline of two men edging their way along the path. Moments later the Tanning brothers disappeared into the darkness. Chet lifted his rifle, contemplated firing a couple of shots over their heads to put an extra scare into them, but decided the wounds in Will's shoulder had given them enough to think about.

Chet knew Dave Tanning would not give up that easily but he had to make it more difficult for him to get people into the valley this way again. He picked up the axe and removed the few trees hanging over the edge of the cliff above the crevice. The next day with the help of John Hart, who was a smaller man, they virtually eliminated the likelihood of someone climbing the wall again. Using the rope abandoned by Will and Alan, Chet lowered John down the cliff where John removed the pins and smashed off the stone footholds with a hammer.

'That should keep them off,' Hart said, as he coiled up the rope.

'I think so too,' replied Chet. 'Even the best climbers would find it difficult.'

Will's left arm had hung limp at his side as he and Alan rode back to the Tanning ranch. Alan had ripped off part of his shirt and stuffed it between Will's shirt and the cuts on his shoulder. They rode slowly, as the jarring of the horse sent waves of pain through Will's shoulder. Dave Tanning stood by his office window and shook his head as he watched his sons ride into the yard. Alan helped Will into the large sitting room and set him on a chair.

Dave Tanning stood at the far end of the room watching one of his staff bandage Will up. Luke walked into the room from outside.

Will leaned back and winced in pain. He turned his head to the right and saw his father in the distance. 'He was waiting for us. Somehow he knew we were coming.'

Dave Tanning nodded. 'You rest, Will. Luke, get over here.'

Luke walked over to his father. 'Yes, Pa?'

'Saddle up a fast horse and get to town. Send the doc out first, then ask around at the stores to see if they're expecting a visit from Mitchell or any of the other ranchers.'

'OK, Pa.'

Luke rode to town and had the doctor ride out immediately. He asked around town and gathered as much information as he could. His report back to his father indicated that there had been no recent sign of any of the ranchers but one man had heard Mitchell inquire about cattle auctions in Ballard City on his second visit to Tanning. The doctor bandaged Will's shoulder. He told Will the cuts were deep but clean and he should rest for a few days.

Dave Tanning was frustrated that Mitchell had again outsmarted him and that his son had nearly died. He still wanted to settle things peacefully and decided to confront Mitchell one last time.

That evening Chet sat with Lisa on the lookout over the trail, the soft wind taking the edge off the hot day.

'We're about ready to move some cattle onto this land. I spoke to the others and we agreed that your pa and I should go to the auction in Ballard tomorrow. It's the last one this year.'

'Are you sure it's safe for you two there? After all, Tanning knows you want cattle and that's one of the places he would expect you to go, seeing that he controls the auction in Tanning.'

'You might be right but we have no choice. We won't be looking for trouble but I can handle Tanning if something happens.'

Lisa moved closer to Chet. 'Can you promise me one thing: if there is trouble will you let Pa help? He's awfully good with his rifle.'

'He is at that. I've watched him practicing. He'll hold his own if there's trouble.'

Later that afternoon Mitchell and

Cullen prepared to leave to inspect the three ranches below the Points on their way to the auction in Ballard City. Steve cleaned and double-checked his rifle while Chet did the same with his twin Colts. Chet watched Steve put on a shoulder holster and slip a small handgun into it.

Cullen saw Mitchell's surprised look and smiled. 'I prefer a rifle but learned a long time ago that they weren't much good in close-in trouble. I keep this handy just in case.'

'I like a man that's prepared,' said Chet. 'We ride in the morning but there's something else I need to talk to you about, Steve.'

Chet got up and walked to the door. He turned around and walked back to the table and sat down again with a nervous look on his face. 'I'm not one for words, Steve, so I'll just say what's on my mind . . . Steve, I'd very much like your permission to ask Lisa to be my wife.'

The serious look on Steve's face

turned into a small smile. 'I have to confess that Susan and I had talked about this possibility for some time. Chet, I know I speak for both of us when I say that we'd be honored to have you as part of our family.'

'Thank you, Steve. I'd be mighty proud to be part of it.' Chet reached out and shook Steve's hand.

'Lisa's out on the porch, Chet. Why don't you join her and tell her that you have our blessing.'

Chet grabbed a cup of coffee and walked out to the front porch where he found Lisa staring out at the peaceful valley framed by the powerful Three Points. He stood beside her and sipped his coffee in silence. Lisa saw Chet uncomfortable for the first time.

'It's such a beautiful valley.' Lisa moved closer to Chet.

'It is at that. Care to join me for a walk?'

'I'd like that.'

Lisa took Chet's arm and they strolled along the clear blue creek and crossed the bridge into the closest pasture. The sound of the water dancing over the stones in the creek provided a calming sound in an already tranquil evening. They strolled along the creek for ten minutes, stopping where it fed into the river.

Chet took Lisa's hand from his arm and it almost disappeared when he enclosed it gently in his big hands. Lisa glanced up at Chet and saw him purse his lips with nervousness. She smiled at seeing such a strong confident man suddenly unsure of himself.

'Lisa, there's something I wish to ask you.' Chet's voice was barely audible.

Lisa stood silently and smiled warmly at the tall man.

'This valley is what I've been dreaming about for going on five years, Lisa, ever since I first heard about it. I'd imagined the green grass blowing in the wind, the cattle grazing in the distance, and the eagles floating overhead. I thought it was everything but I was wrong.' Chet took in a deep breath.

'The fact is my life here would be empty without you by my side. I just got your father's permission and you'd make me the happiest man alive if you'd agree to marry me.'

Lisa locked eyes with Chet. 'Of course I'll marry you, Chet. You're all I think about.'

Chet pulled her close and they kissed. Holding each other, they walked further along the river planning their future in the valley. They returned to the cabin an hour later and found everyone eating apple pie. They passed on the news of their engagement, telling John later. Steve Cullen poured drinks for everyone and they raised glasses in celebration.

The next morning the celebration was replaced with work. Chet and Steve saddled up and rode through the trail out of the valley. They ran into the Hart boys at the Falconer ranch.

'Hi, boys. Good to see you again, Jake,' said Mitchell.

'You too, Mr Mitchell.'

223

'Now you fellows call me Chet. Everything going OK?'

'We had a cow with an injured leg at our ranch but we cleaned and covered the wound,' Jake said. 'Everything else is fine.'

'Good work,' replied Cullen.

Jake pointed toward two men sitting on horses in the east. 'Looks like we have company.'

Mitchell nodded. 'Yes, I saw them ride up. Recognize them?'

'Looks like Dave Tanning on the left.' Cullen squinted into the sun. 'Probably one of his boys with him.'

'You two look like you have things well in hand here.' Chet turned his horse to face the riders silhouetted in the sun. 'I think Steve and I will go have a word with those fellows. You two can put some distance between you and them.'

'We can lend a gun.' Jake patted his pistol.

'I know, but we need you to warn them in the valley if there's trouble,' said Mitchell.

The boys agreed and rode closer to the Points, keeping watch over their shoulders on the way. They stopped well away from the men but close enough to watch them.

Chet and Steve checked their guns and turned south. They rode several hundred yards until they could approach the two riders without facing into the sun. The riders remained sitting on their horses at the top of the rise. As the sun took the two riders out of shadow Mitchell and Cullen approached Dave and Alan Tanning slowly.

'Chet,' said Cullen quietly. 'Keep an eye on that Alan Tanning. He hasn't had a lot of fights but he's very good with a knife and not bad with a gun either.'

'I'll keep my eyes open.'

Dave Tanning sat up straight in his saddle. His hand-tooled saddle reflected his considerable wealth. On the horse beside him sat Alan Tanning. Alan leaned forward in his saddle, his left elbow resting on the pommel, his right hand within easy reach of his tied-down gun. As Mitchell and Cullen neared, the younger Tanning straightened up and adjusted the brim of his hat, instinctively using his left hand.

Mitchell and Cullen rode straight up to them. Dave Tanning looked over at his impatient son and moved his horse forward and to his left, positioning himself in front of his son.

'We need to talk, Mitchell,' drawled Dave Tanning.

'Might at that. I'm listening.' Mitchell spoke to Dave Tanning but kept an eye on Alan.

'What brings you two out here?' said Alan abrasively.

'Just having a look around,' said Chet. 'What brings you out here?'

'Why, we're keeping an eye out for the likes of you,' said Alan.

'Alan, enough!' Dave Tanning glared at his son and then turned his attention back to Chet and Steve. 'Mitchell, I respect a man who wants his way. Fact is, that's how I came to own all this land. But this has to end. Cullen here will tell you: I always get my way. Why don't you get off my valley and head north? Word is there is plenty of land available up there.'

Chet smiled. 'I suppose there is but I like it in the valley.'

Dave Tanning glared back. 'Now I figure you've caused enough trouble in these parts. My patience is getting short. Now get!'

'Why, that's not very neighborly of you, Tanning,' Chet said.

Mitchell noticed Alan move his horse slowly to the left. Dave Tanning never took his eyes off Mitchell and Cullen.

Alan Tanning spit tobacco in front of Chet's horse. 'Mitchell, I don't reckon I'm going to let anybody back talk my pa that way.'

'You fixing to try something?'

'I might just do that you — '

Dave Tanning raised a giant callused hand. 'Easy, Alan. We can surely work this out peacefully.' Tanning turned his gaze to Cullen who sat with his rifle resting diagonally across his saddle. 'Cullen, I don't think it's a good idea to get too close to this fellow. He'll be leaving the area real soon and you don't want things to get any tougher for you and your family.'

'I know what I'm doing. Your days of running the whole show around here are done.'

Dave Tanning's big horse shook its head and shuffled its legs as if it could feel the rider's anger build.

Alan Tanning pulled his horse up close to his father's and whispered in his ear. The elder Tanning shook his head and turned his attention back to Mitchell and Cullen.

'We're going now, but don't think this is the end of it.'

'Don't see things changing, Tanning. My mind's made up,' said Mitchell.

Dave Tanning turned his horse around and waved at his son to follow suit.

Alan Tanning turned his horse around but quickly turned back. 'You two best take what my pa says seriously. If you don't you'll be dealing with me and you won't like the way that'll end.'

Chet and Alan locked eyes. Finally Alan twisted his horse around and rode off with his father toward their ranch.

Mitchell and Cullen waited until the Tannings were out of sight before continuing on to Ballard City. They rode quickly so that they would reach the town by midday and have time to inspect the cattle carefully before the auction the next day. They made only one stop at a spring to water their horses and refill their canteens.

The two main streets of Ballard City contained dozens of horses belonging to other visitors in town for the auction. The saloons overflowed with people. Chet and Steve spent the afternoon wandering though the herds of cattle up for sale the next day. Chet planned to purchase eight hundred head and Steve wanted to expand his herd by three hundred.

The selection varied considerably.

Some cattle looked tired and poorly fed while others looked healthy and fat. The largest number of interested buyers milled around the six or seven groups of strong, healthy young animals.

The crowd of purchasers filed into the town center to eat or have a drink as the sun dropped slowly into the west. Chet nudged Steve and the two ranchers moved away from the few remaining men.

'Have a look over there.' Chet pointed towards the west where a cloud of dust washed over the red sky. 'Looks like there's a late arrival. Let's have a look.'

The newly arrived cowhands collected the cattle at a stream. The cows, dusty and thirsty, caught the eye of both Chet and Steve. They counted just over fourteen hundred head.

'They look healthy Chet, young and strong.'

'I think so, too. We may have an advantage, seeing how they'll be the last ones sold and the other buyers never got a good look at them.'

They checked into a hotel and cleaned up before meeting in the dining room for a much needed meal. The dining room, nearly full, buzzed with conversations about the sale.

'Recognize anybody?' asked Chet.

Steve had been to a couple of sales in Ballard City over the years. 'The few I know ranch just north of us. Good honest men.'

Chet ate the last piece of his apple pie and drained his coffee. 'Why don't we head over to the saloon for a beer before catching some shut-eye?'

'Sounds good to me.'

The two men dropped fifty cents each on the table and walked through the lobby. The sound of a piano greeted them as they entered the smoky saloon. A dozen cowboys stood at the long bar that stretched along the whole north wall, a mirror running along the wall behind it. Opposite the lobby entrance a set of wooden stairs led up to a second floor lined with hotel room

231

doors. Below the second floor walkway a skinny man in a white shirt and red suspenders pounded away on an old piano. Across from the bar, batwing doors led to the street. Poker players played high-stakes games at four tables on each side of the door. With the auction the next day, plenty of money was moving across the felt covered tables.

Mitchell and Cullen studied each face in the room. They bought two beers at the bar and sat at a small table near the piano.

Steve took a sip of beer and pointed it across the room. 'Have a look at the table against the far wall, the fellow wearing the dark shirt.'

Chet looked over. 'Well, I'll be — It's Alan Tanning, and by the look of that stack of chips in front of him he's doing OK?' Chet frowned. 'I'm guessing he knows we're in town. I don't know why he's working so hard at poker and not keeping an eye on us.'

'Typical Tanning, paying someone

else to do the dirty work. Have a look at that stocky man leaning against the second floor railing,' said Steve.

The powerfully built man on the balcony overlooking the saloon cradled a drink in one hand and had a Winchester rifle resting on the railing in front of him, his right hand never far from the trigger. His head seemed on a swivel as it moved back and forth around the room.

'Who is he, Steve?'

'Name's Lance Boulder, a close friend of the Tanning family and as mean as a wildcat. Dave Tanning hires him to watch over him or his sons if they're carrying large amounts of money. He's here to guard Alan and his cash for buying cattle.'

'Looks like he's on the job all right.'

'Yup, and don't trust him a lick. He'd steal from you just as soon as look at you and deny it even if he's caught red handed.'

Chet and Steve finished their beers and ordered a couple more. They sipped the beer and watched Alan Tanning win two more hands.

As the dealer shuffled, Alan looked up at Boulder. The gunman pointed towards Mitchell and Cullen. Alan Tanning's eyes looked where Boulder pointed and spotted the two ranchers. His gaze locked on but his face remained neutral, a sign of a confident man and a good gambler.

Chet sipped beer. 'Have you ever seen Alan Tanning use his guns?'

'I've heard about one time he slapped iron and saw the other, both in Tanning.'

'Clean fights?'

'I hear the first one was straight up but against some drifter bullied into the fight. They say he was mighty slow and Tanning beat him easily.'

'And the second?'

'The second was on the same street six months later. It was against a fellow named Tom Jackson.'

'I've heard of him. They say he was quick.'

'They both were, but Jackson got the worst of it. Tanning was grazed in the leg and Jackson took one in the gut. He died slow and in pain. But' — Cullen drained his beer — 'Chet, I've been around rifles all my life and I swore I heard a rifle shot just before the other two fired. Took a close look at Jackson's wound and it looked too big to be from a handgun. Others say they heard it too but didn't want to say anything against a Tanning. It can make life tough as you and I know.'

'Where was Boulder at the time?'

'He disappeared before the gunfight but reappeared later in the saloon, rifle in hand as usual. Now that you mention it I think he came back to the saloon from the rooms upstairs. Wouldn't surprise me a bit if he gave the edge to Alan.'

'More like a guarantee.'

Mitchell and Cullen had one more beer and paid their bill. They walked through the swinging doors and stood on the boardwalk in front of the saloon.

Cullen smelled pipe smoke and turned to his right where a gray-haired man wearing a bow tie leaned back on a chair, a cloud of smoke rising from his pipe. Harold McCloud pulled the pipe from his mouth and smiled.

'Howdy, Steve.' The man eased his thin frame out of the chair and shook hands with Cullen.

'Good to see you, Harold. It's been too long.'

'That it has.'

'Harold McCloud, this is Chet Mitchell, the man who opened up the valley in the Three Points and the man who'll marry Lisa.'

Chet shook the older man's callused hand.

'Nice to meet you, Mitchell. Quite a feat, getting cattle onto that valley,' said McCloud.

'Thanks. Glad to know you,' replied Chet to the jovial rancher.

'Harold has a large spread a ways north of us. He's one of the bigger suppliers of cattle to the auction,'

Cullen explained. 'In fact, he sold me a few hundred head privately a couple years ago.'

'How'd they turn out, Steve?' asked Harold.

'Real high quality beef. Let us know if you have any more available. The other small ranchers and I have worked out an arrangement where we'll share the valley in the summer and Chet'll keep cattle on our land in the cooler weather.'

'Makes sense.' McCloud put his pipe in his pocket. 'Tell you what, I have another four hundred head I can let you have at eighteen dollars a head. Gives you a break on the price and saves me bringing them here and the sales commission.'

Steve turned to Chet. 'Harold only raises top level steers. I suggest we take them. It's not far out of our way to pick them up on the way back with the cattle we're buying.'

As Mitchell, Cullen and McCloud shook hands Alan Tanning and Boulder left the saloon. They stopped and leered at the three men before moving on.

McCloud laughed. 'I don't mind saying that I don't like those Tannings. Never have.'

Mitchell and Cullen said goodbye to McCloud and the older man joined a group of ranchers gathered on the street.

Steve gestured at McCloud. 'About ten years ago Tanning backed out on a sale to McCloud at the last minute, leaving McCloud short of stock that year. It cost Harold a lot of money and he heard Tanning had laughed about it to people in town. Harold looks skinny but what's there is all muscle. Tanning may have outweighed him by thirty pounds but Harold gave as good as he got. The town of Tanning talked about that fight for months and Tanning gave Harold plenty of room when they came across each other after that.' Steve and Chet decided to call it a night and went up to their room.

11

The auction started at nine the next morning. Chet and Steve got up early and wandered through the cattle. They found two more interesting lots to help reach a total of nine hundred head, including the cattle from McCloud. The buyers gathered around as the auctioneer climbed onto the back of a wagon to start the selling. Chet and Steve talked to a few other ranchers, several shaking their heads and patting Chet on the back when told how Mitchell had gained access to the valley.

The sale moved along quickly, the quality cattle selling for between twenty-two and twenty-four dollars a head. The three lots of interest to Mitchell and Cullen came near the end of the sale. This pleased them as they hoped that most of the other buyers would have already purchased their cattle, allowing them to get the ones they wanted for a good price.

The auctioneer banged down the gavel to open bidding on the first of the lots. Chet did the bidding and was pleased that only one other man showed interest in the cattle. Perhaps they could get the fine steers at twenty dollars or less. The bidding went back and forth, the other bidder growing hesitant as the price neared twenty dollars.

'Nineteen,' shouted Mitchell.

The auctioneer's eyes turned to the other bidder. 'I have a bid of nineteen . . . any other bids . . . do I hear twenty?'

The other bidder shook his head and turned away.

'Very well,' continued the auctioneer. 'It's twenty, going once, going twice . . .' He raised the gavel.

'Twenty,' a bid came from well back in the crowd of ranchers.

'Twenty it is.' The auctioneer's eyes met Chet's. 'What's your bid mister, I have twenty?'

Chet looked over his shoulder but

could not see who had placed the last-second bid. 'Twenty-one.'

'Very good, I have twenty-one.' The auctioneer spoke quickly, trying to maintain the flow of bidding. 'Let's hear twenty-two then . . . twenty-two.'

Harold McCloud walked through the crowd and stood beside Mitchell. 'Chet, it's that skunk Alan Tanning driving up your price. Why don't you push it a few more dollars, then stop? Make him over-pay and take the cows. I'll cover the difference if you get caught paying too much and supply five hundred more head if you can't pick up any for a good price. Let's stick it to that family.'

Chet nodded agreement and McCloud chuckled to himself as he walked away. 'Yes, we'll show those skunks.'

Chet raised his hand. 'Twenty-two.'

'Twenty-four.' Alan Tanning bid quickly, thinking that the two-dollar jump would stop Mitchell and they would get the cows at a good price.

'Twenty-six!' shouted Chet, just as quickly.

'Who does that Mitchell think he is?' Alan said to Boulder. 'I'll fix him, he'll be heading home with nothing.'

'Twenty-eight!' screamed Tanning.

A buzz rolled through the crowd at the bid, well above that of any other cattle of equal quality. Chet listened to the auctioneer plead for another bid but knew he had pushed Tanning far enough.

'Sold!' said the auctioneer. 'Twenty-eight a head.'

Twenty minutes later the last lot of the sale and the last lot of cattle that interested Mitchell and Cullen came up for bid. Again the bidding moved well over a reasonable price and Chet and Alan were the last bidders. Once again Chet pushed Tanning to bid twenty-eight.

Chet looked back at Tanning and smiled. 'Thirty-one.'

A hush fell over the crowd. All eyes fixed on Alan Tanning.

The price was high but Alan wanted to make sure Mitchell went home empty-handed. 'I bid thirty-two a head.'

'Too much for me,' Chet said, when asked by the auctioneer.

The crowd dispersed in a buzz as Chet and Steve walked back to the hotel to gather their gear. Alan Tanning and Boulder leaned against a hitching post outside the hotel with large smiles on their faces as Chet and Steve walked past. Alan Tanning's jaw dropped when he saw them grin right back at them and shake hands with Harold McCloud outside the hotel lobby.

Even Lance Boulder smiled at Alan. 'Looks like they took care of you. Your pa won't be happy that you bought nine hundred head at nearly thirty dollars a head.'

'Shut your mouth, Lance.'

Boulder stopped laughing as he realized the Tannings paid him well and he best behave himself. Alan Tanning stomped up the stairs and into the saloon. Boulder grabbed his rifle that had been leaning against a post and followed him in.

Chet, Steve and Harold sat in the diner drinking coffee.

'That was really something, Chet.' Steve shook his head. 'How did you know Tanning would go that high?'

'The sons may be men but they fear their pa. Since there were so few cattle left for sale I figured Alan thought we were desperate and would go that high and he could impress Dave.'

'Well I know Dave Tanning,' said McCloud, laughing, 'and how he likes to hold onto his money. He won't be happy. No sir, not happy at all.'

'We owe you, Harold,' said Chet.

'Ah, we gave it to Tanning good, that's payment enough. Heck, why don't you tell me about how you figured out a way to the valley and we'll call it even. Dynamite; I'll be damned.' McCloud shook his head.

The next afternoon Chet, Harold and Steve saddled up their horses and joined the dozens of other ranchers heading out of town. There was no sign of Alan Tanning or Lance Boulder. The boards rattled as they crossed the small bridge over the river toward Harold's spread. They turned northwest and rode over to McCloud's sprawling ranch. Thousands of healthy cattle cropping grass greeted them as they entered the rancher's land. The soil and grass were good. From a far distance Chet spotted the huge two-story ranch-house that housed Harold and his large family. The older boys ran the day-to-day operations of the ranch while Harold still enjoyed buying and selling the cattle.

'Why don't you stay for lunch before heading out? Our cook is very good and you can meet the family?' asked Harold.

'I'd like that,' replied Chet.

'Harold, your cook is a legend in these parts. I wouldn't miss it,' added Steve.

They enjoyed a fine meal while some of the hands gathered up the cattle. The quality of the cows pleased Mitchell and Cullen. With three cowboys supplied by McCloud to help move the herd they prepared to start the drive to the valley.

'I wish I could come along and see the valley but I'm a little old for cattle drives.' said Harold.

'You and your family are welcome any time and thanks again.'

As McCloud didn't trust Tanning any more than did Mitchell or Cullen he readily supplied riders who could handle themselves in a fight or with a gun. Each wore a gun and kept a rifle in a scabbard. Chet, Steve and the three riders gathered the cattle early the next morning and moved them across the grassland toward the Three Points, standing majestically on the horizon, gold from the rising sun. With the help of the three experienced cowboys they expected to arrive in the valley within two days.

Chet and Steve rode on opposite sides of the herd, directing them through the undulating prairie and toward the valley. The three others followed, keeping the cows moving and collecting strays. Several miles along they came to a river and drove the cattle eastward, paralleling the fast running water.

An hour later Chet raised his hand and they brought the drive to a stop where the river turned south. A shallow, slow-moving creek cut north from the river and wound its way up to the Points.

They collected fuel for a fire and brewed coffee. The sun provided warmth and good visibility as all five men kept an eye on the horizon for riders. McCloud had provided grub and they ate while the cattle drank the cool water. Then they mounted up and prepared to move the herd across the creek.

The young cattle could not have handled crossing the river but easily made their way across the creek. A couple of smaller steers hesitated but joined the others after a slap with a rope. They followed the creek on the opposite side and made good time, the Points growing taller as each hour passed. As they approached sunset they searched for a place to camp. The sloping edge of the creek valley gave protection from the wind but also provided a multitude of spots for an ambush. Still looking for a secure spot, the drive continued along a narrow area of the embankment onto the relatively flat open range.

'I see some light over that hill to the south.' Chet said, pointing.

Steve nodded and drank from his canteen. 'Looks like sun reflecting in field glasses. We have company all right. And you can bet that it's Tanning.'

Chet moved behind his horse, opposite the people on the far rise and pulled his field glasses out of his saddle-bag. Leaning down a bit, he trained them on the reflected light while keeping himself in shadow under the roan's neck. 'It's them all right. I see both Alan and Boulder. Steve, let's camp here for the night. That hill opposite them gives us a good view with cover from the trees and bushes. We'll alternate watch.'

'I'll take the first watch. I'd sure like to send a couple of pieces of lead past their ears. That would send them back to the Tanning ranch.' Steve tapped his rifle butt.

'OK, I'll go second and get one of the others to take the early watch before we leave.'

One of the McCloud hands could cook, and they had a hearty meal of beef and boiled potatoes. One of the men agreed to spell off Chet at four in the morning.

As darkness fell over the camp Steve slipped up the hill and knelt down between two trees overlooking their small camp. He watched a fire glowing and hundreds of cows eating grass and resting after a long day's walk. The only sound Steve heard was the occasional bawl from a steer.

Chet replaced him well after midnight and settled down in the same place. An hour later he heard a rustling sound behind him. He twisted around and leveled the rifle. Fifty feet away a porcupine looked up and stared at Chet as it trudged through the underbrush. Chet lowered the rifle and got up. The animal moved off as Mitchell looked around the small group of trees and out on the rangeland beyond. Several hours later Coulter, a McCloud hand, replaced Chet, who managed a couple more hours' shut-eye before breakfast.

The sun rose red as the coffee brewed.

'I'm surprised they didn't try anything.' said Chet. 'We should be in the valley before nightfall. Steve, why don't you ride along the other side of that high ridge over there, just high enough to keep an eye on Tanning and Boulder? I'm sure they're still around somewhere. They have to make their move soon and we'd best know which way they'll be coming at us.'

★ ★ ★

Alan Tanning and Boulder rode through trees and came out on the other side of the ridge, half a mile from the herd and riders. They rode to the peak of the ridge and saw two men behind the herd and two others, including Mitchell, on the sides as they moved along the edge of the creek. Across the herd from them they spotted Cullen on another ridge, keeping watch. He had a high vantage point and almost certainly saw them.

'I don't know, Alan,' Boulder frowned. 'I can't see us getting near enough to take down Mitchell and Cullen with five sets of eyes watching. Those are three of the best men from the McCloud crew. I know they aren't afraid of trouble.'

'I've been thinking the same thing, Lance. We need the benefit of surprise to give us an edge and I think I know how we can get it.'

'I'm listening.'

'If we can get at them while they're trapped in the narrow area of their new trail into the valley we can pick them off easily. I know they're watching from above the new valley entrance but if we approach the Points from the south and ride in tight to the trees the lookout won't see us and warn them. Then we hide the horses and set the trap.'

'Let's ride east a ways before we turn south. They'll think we're heading to your ranch.' Boulder's spirits picked up and they prodded their mounts into a gallop.

★ ★ ★

Steve watched Tanning and Boulder ride off. Once out of sight he crested the hill and rode side-by-side with Chet. 'Those two rode off in a hurry, Chet.'

'What direction?'

'Straight east. Maybe to the Tanning ranch.'

'Doubt it. I think they have something planned or they wouldn't have stayed with us this long. I expect they'll double back and try and dry gulch us.'

'There aren't any places between here and the Points that would work — too wide open,' said Steve.

'I'm thinking the same thing. My

guess is that they'll attack in the trees beside the trail up to the new passage. It's the only cover around where those coyotes can get close enough to surprise five men.'

'This could be trouble. That Boulder's one accurate *hombre* with a rifle.' Cullen shook his head.

'I think they'll come at the trail in the shadows and behind the trees and boulders. There's no way John and Nick will spot them if they don't come into the open.' Chet pulled out one of his Colts and checked the action. 'Can you four handle the rest of the drive? I want to go ahead and set up my own surprise for those two.'

'We'll be fine, Chet. You be careful.'

Chet told the other riders of his plan and turned his horse towards the slope to the north. The powerful roan loved to run and climbed the hill with easy strides. He dropped into the shallow wash on the other side of the rise. The horse then hit a full gallop straight towards the north end of the Three

Points. His horse had speed but Tanning and Boulder had a head start and were almost certainly already in the trees.

Chet approached the forest with caution. He came upon the small stream fed by the river flowing nearly straight north from the Points. Chet followed it, occasionally riding right in the stream to stay as low as possible. He stopped half a mile from the trees and left his horse near the stream. He crawled to the top of the rise with his gun in hand. He saw no sign of the two men. Back on his roan, he rode quickly to the edge of the trees. He tied his horse to a bush beside the creek but out of sight in the trees. Reaching up, he pulled his moccasins out of the saddle-bag.

Wearing the soft-bottomed footwear, he quietly entered the bush and moved south. He kept to the trees near the bottom of the Points as they had less brush. He walked on pine needles as much as possible and avoided dry leaves and twigs. Surprise was essential for his plan to work, and with a gunman like Boulder involved, he knew he had only one chance.

As he neared the trail he slowed his step, stopping regularly to listen for the two waiting gunmen. He moved forward in a zigzag pattern to cover as much area as possible, mentally eliminating certain areas. It was unlikely that they would cross the bridge over the gorge, as it was exposed to view from the lookout over the entrance. Chet expected Tanning and Boulder to attempt the strike near the bottom. There they had access to a quick escape if need be. Further up the trail the targets would have access to cover and there were no long straight stretches where all the targets would be in view.

Chet moved slowly down the hill, wary of startling birds or other animals and giving away his position. Now, within easy sight of the trail, he crouched down and crawled along the ground. He came upon a pile of logs he had cleared from the trail. On the other side of the pile he had collected brush and rocks, forming a natural fence to keep cattle confined to the trail. He reached up and put a little weight on the first few logs. Finding them secure, he climbed up and studied the area through the tangled pile of brush and branches on the other side.

He was preparing to climb onto the next log when he heard a noise behind some enormous rocks on the opposite side of the trail. The cracking sound was barely audible. Was it an animal foraging for food? Was it a falling branch? Chet stood dead still. If it were Tanning and Boulder, who had experience in the woods, they would not only stay still but would watch closely for anyone who might have noticed their noise. Even behind the cover of the piled branches, movement on his part might be spotted with a good set of eyes.

Ten minutes passed. Chet knew that when hiding out ten minutes seemed like an hour. He fought the urge to move, even though remaining at the top of the log pile left him vulnerable to a bullet. He wanted to maintain his vantage point should it turn out that Tanning or Boulder had made the noise. Twenty minutes later his patience paid off.

The top of a black hat briefly appeared over one of the rocks, a hat like that worn by Lance Boulder. A second movement caught Mitchell's eye, this time the slight adjustment of a rifle barrel resting in the 'V' between the two six-foot high rocks.

Chet mulled over his options. He slowly eased himself down behind the logs and looked at the escape routes behind him. Just uphill, two large trees lay over a dip in the earth, the narrow path indicating it was an animal route. Although dead, the trees had many branches protruding the full length of the trunks, preventing easy passage. Once through the gap on the other end he could escape with no chance of anyone getting a clear shot at him. This would make the odds even, or perhaps favor Mitchell with his experience in the woods. He had his chance.

Chet slowly raised his rifle over the logs, resting it on a thicker branch in the brush to provide stability. The hat moved back and forth behind the rocks, only visible through the small gap between. Mitchell sat patiently, his rifle trained on the opening, waiting for the man to move by again. The hat showed above the rock to Mitchell's right, only a sliver of the top exposed. It disappeared briefly then reappeared, this time from further back of the boulder, exposing Boulder's head and part of his chest. Chet steadied the rifle and slowly squeezed the trigger. The blast echoed through the trees. Chet lifted his head and saw Boulder sprawl backwards dead, a red bloom spreading on his throat.

Mitchell had not seen Alan Tanning with Boulder and needed to move to a more secure position as this one was now compromised by the rifle shot. He dipped behind the logs, smoking rifle in hand. Crawling quickly along the ground, Chet flipped onto his back to slide through the animal path under the dead trees. The big man just fit under the logs, his chest rubbing on the rough bark. Near the other side of the logs Chet felt a tug on the rifle. He stopped, using up precious escape time, and tugged on the butt of the weapon. It would not move. He slid his hand further down the rifle and found a long, thin branch had slipped into the trigger guard. In the tight confines under the logs Mitchell could not remove the branch and did not have enough room to snap the branch. He knew he had little time, so left the rifle and slid through the path, exiting on the other side.

He flipped on to his hands and knees and put his palms on the ground to push his body up so he could make for the thick trees up the hill. As he started to lift himself he heard a shot ring out.

Not from the rocks on the other side of the trail, but from the opposite direction. A searing pain in his left arm sent him tumbling back to the ground. He stayed on the ground and crawled behind a thick bush just to his left. He looked at his arm and saw a tear in his shirt, soaked in blood.

'You're mine, Mitchell,' Alan Tanning shouted from a hidden position above Mitchell. 'Now stand up and take it like a man.'

Tanning fired into the brush three times. One deflected off branches while two got through, the second plowing into the ground in front of Mitchell, sending dust flying into his face. Mitchell rolled to his right to better cover where thin but numerous trees stood between him and the flying bullets. It was better cover, but still not solid. He sat up and took a moment to look at his arm. The lead had ripped open the skin but had missed the bone. He ripped a strip of cloth off his bandanna and tied it tightly around his arm, stopping the bleeding.

The cover, albeit low, spanned fifteen feet from the spot where Mitchell sat to the other end of the brush and small trees. Tanning's talking had given away his position. He sat perched in a grove of trees seventy feet up the hill. Better cover for Mitchell, in heavier trees, meant a twenty-foot run through a clearing. Behind him the logs blocked his path and he knew Tanning had a clear view of it. The heavy branches on top of the logs made climbing over too slow. Chet needed time to make a run for cover, as eventually Tanning would surely fire through the thin trees and brush.

Chet checked his guns; both were loaded. He took off his hat and put a fist-sized rock inside, securing it in place by wrapping the remainder of his bandanna around the hat. With the hat in his right hand and his Colt in the left, he dug his right foot into the ground to help get a good running start. Tanning fired blindly, bullets ricocheting off the thin trees and bush. A couple shots missed

Mitchell by inches. Tanning clearly knew where he was. The sun streamed through the high trees in beams of yellow behind Tanning's hiding spot, making Chet's visibility far from perfect.

Tanning fired in groups of three, so Chet waited and risked the next hail of bullets. The third shot whistled past his left ear. Chet stood part way up and fired five shots in the direction of Alan. He ducked back down and threw the hat towards the top of the bush well to the right, the end of the bandanna fluttering. Pushing off on his right foot, he ran at full speed past the end of the brush and tree cover. As he ran, Tanning fired three more times at the area where the hat had appeared above the brush. Alan Tanning quickly realized the diversion and saw Mitchell moving out of the corner of his eye.

'I got you now, Mitchell!' shouted Tanning as he swung his rifle to his right, aiming at Mitchell as he ran across the open area in a crouch. Tanning pulled the trigger. Chet ducked as low as he could as the rifle spit fire. Alan had little time to aim but fired three times, clean misses because the shots were high. Alan slowed down and took a breath. He aimed again and took two more shots. The first cut through Chet's shirt as it flapped behind him. The second splintered the side of a tree on the edge of the grove as Mitchell dove into the heavy cover.

'Don't matter what you do, Mitchell; I've got you. I saw you only have your handguns. They aren't any match for my rifle. You best just throw out your guns and walk out of there with your hands raised.' Tanning fired three more shots into the trees.

Chet used the stubborn arrogance of Tanning against him. He tossed some pebbles to his right so Alan would think he was still there. As Tanning talked, Mitchell quickly and silently moved further along the cover to his left. With the moccasins muffling his steps Mitchell climbed the hill to Tanning's right. Three more shots pounded into the trees where Chet had been a minute earlier. Moving as if on air, Chet worked his way farther left so he remained behind at least partial cover as he approached the same level of the hill as that occupied by Tanning. Alan stopped firing into the trees below him. This made Chet extra cautious and slowed him down as he moved above and behind Tanning.

Alan Tanning didn't know if Mitchell was wounded, dead or had gotten away. Clearly, he couldn't coax Chet to speak and give away his position. Alan reloaded his rifle and checked the position of his handgun. Had Boulder taken a bullet? If he hadn't, why wasn't he coming to help him? Tanning sat quietly but grew increasingly nervous while he waited, as the arrival of Cullen and the others would increase Mitchell's chances and put himself in danger.

Mitchell edged along the hill, watching each step carefully. He stopped ten minutes later and took up a position between two large trees. The branches gave solid cover and the high position gave a good view. Between the branches he systematically scanned the area in the direction from which Tanning had shot. The trees and rocky terrain gave plenty of cover, but movement in a small clearing just east of Tanning's previous position caught Chet's eye. Here Alan Tanning crouched in wait, his rifle gripped tightly and his head darting from left to right. Tanning even glanced uphill a few times but never spotted Mitchell in his heavily pro-tected position. Alan's spot had an excellent view of a long stretch of the trail and the surrounding area. Tanning had piled up rocks and logs on the side facing the trail, a small fort.

Chet rubbed his chin as he watched his adversary search for him and grow more agitated as each minute passed. From Chet's high vantage point the upper part of Boulder's body was visible. In a small clearing below Boulder stood their horses. Chet had Alan Tanning easily covered, even with a Colt from thirty feet away. Mitchell sat still and watched the area for another five minutes, watching carefully for others who might be working with Tanning.

He saw nothing and decided to deal with Alan Tanning face to face. He surveyed the lie of the land between himself and Tanning. Loose rocks and branches on the steep embankment directly between them meant poor footing and a risk of exposure in the open. The trail sat a short distance to Chet's left, far too exposed from Tanning's perch. Chet started out on the only option remaining, to return part way back in the direction he had come and enter the small clearing through the trees on the same level of the hill that held Tanning. Mitchell stopped frequently on his slow journey back down the hill, keeping a close watch on Tanning, who remained behind his fortress. Progress slowed when he saw Alan start to watch more frequently in all directions.

Looks like he's really starting to worry, thought Mitchell. *So much the better*.

As Chet reached the same level as that of Alan, he briefly lost sight of him behind a thick grouping of trees. He slowed his pace as he moved to the edge of the trees, the clearing just visible in front of him. As Chet moved part way out into the open he saw Alan's focus primarily stayed on the trail. The overconfidence of a Tanning wouldn't let him believe that someone could move around without being spotted.

Mitchell walked out into the open, stood up straight and squared himself to Tanning, his Colts loaded and ready. 'Drop that rifle, Tanning, or it'll be the last thing you do.'

Alan Tanning froze, his knuckles white from his tight grip on the Winchester. 'You best not fire. I'm not alone. I'll bet Boulder has you in his sights as we speak.'

'You'd lose that bet, Tanning. Your

friend is dead, lying behind the rocks from where he was setting up his ambush. Now drop that gun. I won't ask again.'

'Just get off our land.' Alan Tanning's voice cracked with anger. 'You're not welcome here.'

'I think that you're the one not — '

As Mitchell spoke Alan spun around and leveled his rifle at waist height. Mitchell drew, his hand a flash. Two shots hit Tanning in the chest, killing him before he had a chance to pull the trigger. Chet holstered his gun and walked over to the dead man. He bent to pick up the rifle when a shot rang out, digging into a tree to Mitchell's right. Chet fell flat on the ground and rolled to the left behind a low log. Two more shots Mitchell recognized as from a rifle drove into the log beside him, sending splinters into his face. Mitchell was happy to have the small fortress built by Tanning as cover. He crawled closer to the logs and rocks where he took a moment to clear the small pieces of wood from his eyes.

'That was my brother you just bushwhacked Mitchell!' yelled Will Tanning from on top of an outcropping of soil near the edge of the trees.

'I gave him fair warning, Will, just like I'm giving to you. Get off my land or you'll have the same fate as Alan.'

'Your land? You stole it from my pa and you're going to pay with your life.'

'I didn't think this was your style, Will. A man has to be mighty yellow to kill someone without looking him in the eyes.'

'I'm not yellow and you're going to find that out on Monday. You come to Tanning and we'll settle this like men. Does that sound yellow to you?'

'I'll meet you, but not at Tanning. We'll deal with this at Ballard City. That is if you aren't afraid and don't show.'

'Ballard City it is. But I'm not leaving without my brother's body.'

'You back away and I'll tie these two onto their horses and send them down the trail.'

Chet sat still listening. He heard leaves crunch and branches snap. He peeked through some trees and saw Will Tanning make his way down the hill and out to the grassland. He disappeared over a knoll and reappeared shortly with a horse in tow. Chet remained still a little longer in case one of the Tannings or a hired gun was still on the mountainside. Five minutes later he got to his feet and carried Alan Tanning's body to the trail. He did the same with Boulder's. The horses spooked a little but soon let Mitchell lead them to the trail where he tied the bodies over the saddle. He swatted the horses and they walked down the trail and onto the open prairie. Will Tanning gathered their reins and tied them to his horse. He mounted up and started for home, taking a couple of looks back on his way.

Mitchell thought Will Tanning was through talking but the stubborn man stopped and yelled over his shoulder, 'I'll spit on your grave on Monday afternoon, Mitchell!'

Chet only wanted to live in peace in the valley with Lisa Cullen, but didn't like to back down from a challenge. He watched Tanning ride slowly away from the Points with two more dead men draped over a saddle, this time including kin. The confrontation with Will, the fastest gun in the Tanning family, was inevitable.

12

Chet's thoughts turned to Lisa. He had finally found the land for which he had longed and the happiness of the love of a good woman. Still — he had to put his life on the line, even though the difference between life and death went beyond speed in a gunfight. A gun jamming in the holster or misfiring, or the glint of sunlight distracting the shooter, had sent many a good shot to an early grave.

Mitchell came back to the present when he saw Will Tanning abruptly turn to his left and cross a fast-moving creek. The crossing was dangerous, especially with two horses carrying dead men in tow. The change in direction also took him well off the shortest route home. Chet scanned the horizon, his eyes locking on a brown haze rising from the ground. It spread like a sunrise in the area where Tanning had been. The dome of brown sky grew and grew. A black spot on the ground under it also grew wider by the second. The cattle! The herd soon formed a dark line spreading across the crest of the rise.

★　★　★

Tanning also saw the approaching herd and urged his horse to go faster as the dark line moved nearer. He had seen enough trouble for one day and didn't wish others to see the body of a Tanning draped dead over a saddle. Will's anger and frustration grew each time he saw the cows move towards the rich grassland of the hidden valley. Once again he had let down his family and himself. The thought of Lisa Cullen with another man infuriated him, especially that man being Chet Mitchell. He expected he'd have trouble sleeping between then and Monday, anxious to get even with Mitchell. The horse reared up briefly and surged forward as Will angrily dug in his spurs.

★ ★ ★

Chet went to where his rifle had snagged on the branches of the dead tree and freed it. Then he ran back to his roan and raced along the edge of the trees at the bottom of the Three Points, jumping rocks and logs on the way. He arrived as the four men gathered the cattle in preparation for the push up the trail. Steve Cullen was guiding two straying cows back to the herd on the far end as Chet rode up.

'Good to see you're in one piece, Chet,' said Steve.

'Wish it were true.' Chet showed Steve the dried blood on his left arm. 'Alan Tanning and Boulder were waiting in ambush. I'm grazed but it's not serious.'

'And them?'

'Boulder is dead — should have kept his head down. Alan Tanning as well:

took two in the chest. Will showed up and tried to finish me off. We'll be meeting in Ballard City on Monday. Will has the bodies of his brother and Boulder with him; carrying home dead bodies is getting to be a habit with them.'

'Stubborn bunch those Tannings. But they can't be trusted. I'm coming along to watch your back in Ballard City.'

'Obliged. They won't give up easily. Meanwhile, let's get these cattle into the valley.'

Chet and Steve joined the McCloud riders and started the drive up the trail. Mitchell led the way and the other four pushed the cattle to follow. The cows slowly poured into the narrow passage like water into a funnel. Pride swelled in Mitchell as his months of work were finally paying off. The cattle moved smoothly up the trail, past the spot where he had had the shootout with Will and Boulder and along the wandering path. At the bridge over the gorge Chet slipped a railing off the east side of the trail on the upper side and pulled the roan into a small clearing. He replaced the rail and sat tall on the horse, watching the cattle cross the bridge. The fences and heavy bush continued to keep the cattle on the trail. At the lookout Lisa and John Hart smiled down at the snake-shaped line of cattle moving toward the valley.

At last the end of the long line of cattle and riders crossed the bridge. Chet removed the railing and joined Cullen and the other three men on the trail.

The McCloud cowhands looked up in awe as the new opening grew in front of them.

'If that don't beat all,' said Coulter. 'I wouldn't have believed it if I hadn't seen it.'

The men moved the cattle into an area to the south of the cabin and over one of the bridges. The cattle settled in to graze the rich green grass.

Chet removed his hat and wiped the sweat from his brow, watching as the cattle grazed. 'That's a mighty fine sight.'

'It sure is,' said Cullen.

'Steve, first thing in the morning we'll brand these and then bring up some more from yours and the other ranches.'

'Meanwhile, you five look like you could use a good meal.' Lisa smiled up at Chet and her father.

'Hi, Lisa,' Chet smiled. 'Sure could.'

Lisa saw the blood on Chet's sleeve as he dismounted. She removed the bandanna and inspected the wound. 'Why, you've been shot, Chet!'

'Just a scratch. I've had worse.'

'Well, we have to clean that up right away.' Lisa took Chet by the other arm and led him towards the cabin.

'I'll look after your horse,' Steve said.

In the cabin Lisa cleaned Chet's wound while Susan prepared a hearty meal. They ate well and everyone talked, although Chet and Steve said little.

Susan and Lisa noticed their quiet demeanor.

'Chet, Pa, what's wrong?' asked Lisa.

Chet explained the confrontation at the bottom of the trail and the challenge made by Will Tanning.

'Chet,' said Lisa with shock on her face. 'Are you going to face him?'

'Have to, Lisa. This has gone on long enough. It's time to settle it.' Chet placed his hand on Lisa's. 'But I can make you a promise. When this is done I'll settle down to ranching.'

Tears ran down Lisa's cheeks.

Steve looked up from his meal and across at his wife. 'Susan, I don't trust those Tannings one bit. I'm going along with Chet to watch his back.'

'I understand, Steve,' said Susan. 'But please be careful, both of you.'

'Count on me too, Chet,' Falconer said. 'I'll be there. We're in this together.'

Coulter put his fork on his plate. 'Harold told us to stay around and help if there's trouble from those skunks. I reckon this counts. We'll help John Hart watch over this place in case Tanning tries something while you're in Ballard City.'

Over the next few days, with the help of the McCloud men, the cattle in the valley were branded and put out to graze. Chet stood back and watched with pride as the cows cropped the swaying green grass. The nine hundred head seemed small in the massive valley.

Falconer, Cullen, Hart, and one of the McCloud men rounded up cattle from some of the drier areas of the other ranches and herded them into the valley. On the last trip back with cattle from Cullen's ranch, Steve noticed a big man on horseback watching from a distant hill. The man stayed in the shadow of a tree but Cullen recognized Dave Tanning. Cullen reined in his horse and watched his neighbor. Tanning stood on his land at a point where the properties joined. He saw Cullen eyeing him and after a short delay to make an unspoken point, turned and moved back towards his ranch.

John Hart rode up to Cullen. 'He can't be happy.'

'No, he isn't, but we have to work together to survive here.'

They joined the other riders and drove the cattle into the valley. It was Sunday, and that night the mood turned somber at the evening meal. Chet sat quietly beside Lisa as the conversation touched on things ranging from the weather to the few sick cows in the barn. Nobody talked about the trip to Ballard City the next day for the showdown with Will Tanning.

Mitchell looked around the table at the concerned faces and tried to lighten the mood by talking about the good years ahead, now that all four ranchers had plenty of grass and water. But he found it difficult to sway everyone's thoughts away from the next day.

'Lisa, would you join me for a walk?' Chet stood up.

'I'd like that. I could use the air.'

'If you'll excuse us.' Chet opened the door and followed Lisa out into the cool evening air.

They walked hand-in-hand in silence

along the winding stream. Near a tall pine tree Chet stopped and looked at the reflection of the moon in the water. Lisa's eyes fixed on Chet's face; a tear glistened on her right cheek.

Chet looked at her and smiled. He wiped away the tear. 'I can't guarantee that I'll be back tomorrow Lisa, but I'm not afraid of Will Tanning or anyone else. I've battled uphill my whole life. When my pa died they said I wouldn't last a week gold mining. I lasted years and did pretty well. Everyone thought there was no way to get cattle into this valley. It took a lot of planning and hard work but I did it.' Chet swept his hand around the valley. 'I've only seen one thing more beautiful than this valley . . . and that's you, Lisa.'

'Oh, Chet.' Lisa threw her arms around him.

'This is tough country and some-times we have to do things we don't like. But don't bet against me, Lisa.'

'I won't Chet, I won't.'

'That's good.' Chet hesitated. 'Lisa,

this valley would seem empty without you. I hope you realize how much I love you.'

'I do, Chet, and I love you too.'

'I'll look after Will Tanning tomorrow, and have your pa and Nick there to make sure things are fair. Then we'll start our new life together on this very land.'

Chet and Lisa hugged and kissed before joining the others in the cabin.

Early the next morning Chet, Steve and Nick cleaned their weapons and ate breakfast. Twenty minutes later they saddled up and rode through the exit. Halfway to Ballard City Nick Falconer left them and headed north at a gallop, intending on entering the town separately and unseen. None of the three was prepared to trust the Tannings for a second.

Chet and Steve rode into town at ten in the morning, not quite sure what to expect. They found the streets a beehive of activity, with no shortage of pointing and whispering.

'Can't say if Tanning is here but it sure looks like the word has reached town,' Steve said.

'Sure does,' Chet nodded.

As they rode along Main Street, mothers busied themselves shuffling their children indoors. Chet tossed the young man at the livery stable a coin and he took their horses. He rubbed them down and fed them grain.

Chet turned to Steve after the stable hand walked away. 'Isn't that Will Tanning's mount in the first stall?'

'It is at that.'

Chet and Steve walked across the street and into the dining room where they ordered coffee. As the waitress brought the coffee, Harold McCloud walked in and sat across from them. 'Mind if I join you?'

'Not at all, Harold. Thanks for the use of your hands. They're good men,' said Mitchell.

'My pleasure. I saw Will Tanning ride into town alone, but I suggest you don't trust him.'

'I have my back covered.' Chet gestured to Steve.

'Fine, fine. You both be careful.' McCloud got up and shook Chet's hand. 'I'll buy you a drink this afternoon.'

Chet nodded and McCloud shook Cullen's hand before he left the room. Chet sipped his coffee, unwilling to listen to the talk and whispers from the other tables although he could see the pointing and head shaking. They ordered steaks and had nearly finished when the lobby door swung open. The waitress was just coming out of the kitchen with the coffee pot when she saw Will Tanning at the door. She walked back into the kitchen and closed the door. The man and wife at a table at the other end of the room jumped up and left through the door to the street.

Will Tanning leaned on the door jamb and stared at Mitchell. 'Well: you came. I guess you're not as yellow as they say you are.'

'Care to find out right now?'

'Oh, we'll find out; we'll find out at one o'clock. Don't be late.' Tanning left the room as quickly as he had entered.

Mitchell and Cullen finished their second cups of coffee slowly and got up from their chairs. Chet nodded at Steve, who left through the lobby door. Mitchell set a coin on the table and walked out the other door onto the boardwalk. People moved aside as he approached.

The sun sat a bit to the south, a position that could affect the shooter at the north end of the street. He crossed the street and entered the general store. From the front window he looked across at the three-story hotel from which he had just exited. In full view on the second-floor corner balcony sat Steve Cullen, his trusty rifle on his lap. The storekeeper didn't approach Mitchell, aware that the man was deep in thought. Chet remained focused on the street as one o'clock neared.

In a saloon midway down the street Will Tanning stood at the bar. An old man sat passed out at a table with a long-empty beer in front of him. The only other person in the saloon, the bartender, cleaned glasses at the far end of the bar. The clock at the far end of the room showed five minutes to one.

Will drained his whiskey and stood up straight. He walked to the exit and pushed open the batwing doors. As he stood on the boardwalk a man approached him and whispered something. Will nodded. Chet watched this from the darkness of the general store. Will's eyes turned toward the store and seemed to lock on those of his opponent in the dark room. A wry smile crossed Will's face and he walked down onto the street. He centered himself and faced in the direction of the general store, the sun behind him. The general store and Mitchell were a block down the street in front of him.

Chet looked at the clock behind the counter. It showed four minutes to one. He adjusted the position of his twin

Colts and turned toward the door. A lady outside saw him approach and scurried out of his way. The shade of the roof over the boardwalk covered him as he walked one more block north. He scanned the windows, doorways and alleys as he walked, but saw no one suspicious, only shopkeepers.

Across the street the barber shop and doctor's office faced Mitchell. The barber shop sat empty, the barber on a chair in front. Beside him sat a man with half his face covered in shaving cream; no one wanted to miss the action. Mitchell took two steps down from the walkway and put his right foot on the dirt street. Shutters slammed and a din of conversation filled the street. Chet stepped forward, one foot after the other, eyes focused on the buildings on the opposite side of the street. He crossed the center of the street. Chet kept up the steady pace until he reached the boardwalk on the other side of the street and continued straight into the doctor's office.

Heads shook and arms went up. What had Mitchell done? Had he turned yellow? Will Tanning stood halfway down the street with a puzzled look on his face. He waited. Everyone waited.

The big clock above the bank showed one minute to one and everyone watched the doctor's office for the appearance of Chet Mitchell.

'Mitchell, you cowardly dog, get out here!' shouted Will Tanning as the clock neared one. 'Where are you?'

'I'm right here, Tanning,' said Mitchell.

Will Tanning looked over his shoulder to find Chet Mitchell at the opposite end of the street. 'What the — ?'

Chet had walked straight through the doctor's office and out the back door. He took the three minutes before the top of the hour to walk down the next street and pass between two buildings to arrive at the other end of Main Street. From between the buildings he had seen that Cullen had left the balcony. As planned, Steve now knelt on the flat roof above the balcony of the hotel, his rifle at the ready.

Cullen studied the street carefully. He had selected the roof of the hotel as it was the tallest building in Ballard City. From this high vantage point he saw no one on the other rooftops. He then concentrated on open windows, open doors, and other spots where a shooter might position himself.

Movement caught his eye. Across the street from his rooftop perch he saw a rifle poke out from the second-floor window over the feed store. It first pointed at the doctor's office into which Chet had vanished. When Mitchell made his appearance at the other end of the street the barrel pulled back and reappeared at a window directly across from Cullen and close enough to the corner to get a direct shot at Mitchell. The room above the feed store was filled with crates and sacks, some covering much of the window areas.

The street was narrow and Cullen was no more than thirty feet from the gunman.

Steve brought his head down to his rifle sight and took aim. In the darkness of the room he saw the face of Dave Tanning at the other end of the rifle. 'Drop the rifle, Dave. We want a fair fight!' Steve called out just loud enough for Dave Tanning to hear. Chet Mitchell and Will Tanning, just down the street, couldn't hear the conversation.

Dave Tanning looked up from his rifle and sneered at Steve. 'You two think you can outsmart a Tanning. We've been playing these games for years. Before you do something you'll regret you may want to have a look behind you.' Dave Tanning's sneer turned to a smile.

Cullen kept his rifle pointed at Dave Tanning and took a look behind him. Luke Tanning stood there with a gun pointed at him.

'Drop the rifle, Cullen. Do it now,' said Luke.

Cullen looked back at Dave Tanning,

making sure he didn't have his rifle pointed in his direction.

Luke Tanning moved a step closer. 'Pa, I've got him covered.'

As Luke spoke the last word he winced in pain and fell onto the roof. A knife stuck through his ribs and right through his heart, killing him instantly. Nick Falconer stood beside the large brick chimney in the middle of the roof, a second knife in his right hand and a gun in his left.

'I've looked after this coyote, Steve,' Falconer said.

Cullen looked back at Dave Tanning and saw a look of shock on the face of the older man. 'Might be a good idea for you to drop that weapon, Tanning, otherwise you're finished.'

Dave Tanning staggered away from the window and disappeared into the dark interior of the room. His mind was barely able to comprehend the death of two of his sons. Cullen, rifle at the ready, studied the shadowy depths of the room.

'Cullen, you and Falconer are as much to blame for my trouble as Mitchell. Now you've killed my boy! Rot in Hell!' yelled Dave Tanning.

Flashes of light exploded through the middle window. Bullets sailed past Steve's head. Dave Tanning had taken refuge deep in the shadows at the back of the store, out of sight but still with a view of the street and Chet Mitchell. Cullen concentrated on the windows. He expected that a wily man like Dave Tanning would move from the spot where he had just fired.

A glint of light from Tanning's rifle barrel in the window next to the door showed his position. Cullen did not hesitate. Three quick shots spaced out ten inches apart covered the whole opening. Dave Tanning staggered forward into the light streaming in from the street side window, blood flowing from a wound in his gut. The rifle he carried fell to the floor as his hands moved instinctively to his midsection. He stumbled to his left, briefly out of sight behind a pile of crates. He fell through another window facing the main street, crashing onto the ground beside some horses. Both Chet Mitchell and Will Tanning watched as Dave Tanning crashed to the ground.

Will Tanning took two steps towards his father.

Dave Tanning raised a blood-soaked hand that stopped his son. 'Will!' gasped Dave Tanning, a grimace on his face. 'Son, I'm done. Do the family proud and kill that snake Mitchell. He's the one that caused all this. He's the one who caused — ' Dave Tanning's eyes closed for the last time and his head fell to the boardwalk.

Will slowly turned around and faced Mitchell. 'Mitchell, if you think your little trick will stop me getting revenge for my family you're wrong, dead wrong!'

Will pulled down his hat brim to help block the glare of the sun. He took three steps backwards, his hands at the ready. Chet and Will already stood a good distance apart and it puzzled Chet that Tanning would move further back. As soon as Tanning's foot hit the ground on the third step he threw himself down and to his right, turning sideways at the same time. Landing on his left knee, he gave Mitchell a smaller target. As he fell to the ground he gripped his gun and pulled it out of the holster.

As Tanning turned and dropped, Mitchell's instincts kicked in and his hands dropped to his Colts. The guns came up in a blur, followed their target, and spit fire. Tanning's gun lined up on Mitchell's body just as Mitchell's bullets drove into his chest. Tanning's body twitched, sending his gun barrel upwards as his finger pulled the trigger. The bullet flew past Chet's right ear. Tanning slumped to both knees, his left hand grasping his chest, the gun dangling from his right hand. The gun fell to the ground as Tanning curled up into a ball and collapsed, dead. Chet slipped his Colts into his holsters and stood silently while the crowds gathered around the bodies of Dave and Will Tanning. Chet hoped this would be the last time he'd ever *have to use his guns.*

Cullen and Falconer walked out of the hotel. Two hotel employees carried Luke Tanning's body out and placed it on the ground next to his brother. The undertaker knelt over Dave Tanning's body up the street.

'Don't know why some people get greedy to the point they'd rather risk death than get along,' Mitchell sighed.

'I don't know either,' replied Cullen. 'I know things around the Three Points won't be the same with all of the Tannings dead. I hope peace wins out.'

The three friends walked silently up the street and climbed onto their horses. They rode quickly, knowing that the others would want to know what had happened. Without having to look over their shoulders for trouble from the Tannings the prairie seemed brighter. Even the trail into the valley seemed more comfortable with the hoof marks from the horses and cattle in the soil. As they cantered up to the bridge over the gorge they looked up and saw everyone standing on the lookout. Chet saw Lisa on the left; the sun glowed brightly behind her. The men on the trail waved back and were greeted with handshakes and hugs when they entered the valley. The smiles on the faces reflected the promise of a bright future. Peace had finally come to the area, though sadly, it had come at the price of many lives.

Many changes came to the valley over the next few months. The main one was a larger house at the opposite end of the valley, built after the wedding of Lisa and Chet. The house had plenty of room for a large family. The original cabin became the home of Steve and Susan Cullen. They worked closely with their daughter and new son-in-law to build a healthy life and a large herd, a dream they all shared.

They kept the Cullen land and added to it with the purchase of nearby land from the sale of the Tanning property.

Falconer and Hart also bought parcels of land from the same sale. Other ranchers moved in as well, all with similar-sized land holdings. The community of Tanning, renamed Graceville, thrived with Dave Tanning's tight control gone. More stores opened and families moved in. Churches and schools sprang up, helping to develop a more peaceful community.

Lisa joined her husband on the veranda of their house and watched the white clouds pass overhead. She took his arm and held it tight. 'A wonderful morning, isn't it?'

Chet smiled down at Lisa. 'There's never been one better.'

THE END